THE CASE: Find var[...] Trumbull.

CONTACT: Millionaire Alice Faulkner, grandmother of the girl.

SUSPECTS: Ross Rafferty, ambitious chairman of Windward Fidelity. He's upset about his recent divorce from Lisa's mother, Diana, but would he do Lisa any harm?

Mitsuo Kaimonsaki, Windward Fidelity's president. He was the last person to see Lisa before she vanished.

Amy Sorenson, Windward Fidelity's vice-president. Is she loyal to the bank or is she up to something else?

Lester Jarman, Windward Fidelity's retired co-founder. He has loads of money already. Is he greedy enough to betray his old bank?

COMPLICATIONS: Strange "accidents" are happening to Nancy and her companions as they search for Lisa. All clues point to a "Malihini Corporation." But just what—or who—is the Malihini Corporation?

Books in The NANCY DREW™ FILES Series

THE NANCY DREW FILES
CASE • 23

SINISTER PARADISE

Carolyn Keene

AN ARCHWAY PAPERBACK
Published by SIMON & SCHUSTER
New York London Toronto Sydney Tokyo Singapore

An Archway paperback
first published in Great Britain
by Simon & Schuster Ltd in 1992
A Paramount Communications Company

**Simon & Schuster Ltd
West Garden Place
Kendal Street
London W2 2AQ**

NANCY DREW, AN ARCHWAY PAPERBACK
and colophon are registered trademarks of Simon & Schuster Inc.

THE NANCY DREW FILES is a trademark
of Simon & Schuster Inc.

Simon & Schuster of Australia Pty Ltd
Sydney

A CIP catalogue record for this book is
available from the British Library

ISBN 0-671-71639-5

Printed and bound in Great Britain by
HarperCollins *Manufacturing*

SINISTER PARADISE

Chapter

One

"OH, NANCY, CAN you believe this place?" Bess Marvin climbed up the pool ladder, water streaming off her. "I feel as though I've died and gone to heaven!"

Nancy Drew leaned against the diving board. Trade winds stirred her reddish blond hair. "It's a big change from River Heights, Bess, I'll admit that."

"They're probably knee-deep in snow back home." Bess plucked a fluffy towel from the deck chair. "Coming to Hawaii was a *great* idea."

"Too bad it's not a pleasure trip," George Fayne remarked. She stood beside the pool, vigorously toweling her dark hair. "And by the way,

1

Bess, you pronounce it *Huh-wah-ee*, not *Huh-why-ee*."

Nancy heard the tapping of high heels on the patio tiles. Turning, she saw their hostess, Alice Faulkner, heading their way. Mrs. Faulkner was a slim, aristocratic woman in her early seventies, with soft white hair and penetrating eyes. Nancy's mother's family had been very friendly with the Faulkners, and Mrs. Faulkner kept in touch periodically after Nancy's mother died.

The day her granddaughter disappeared, Mrs. Faulkner had phoned Nancy in River Heights and asked her to help locate her. Sixteen-year-old Lisa Trumbull had mysteriously disappeared from school on Friday. Mrs. Faulkner feared that the girl had run away.

Mrs. Faulkner's polite smile flashed at Nancy, then at Ned Nickerson, Nancy's boyfriend, who stood beside the pool ladder. "Aren't you two going swimming?"

"I would, only I left my suit back on the *Kahala*," Ned replied ruefully.

The *Kahala* was their temporary home in Honolulu. It was a fifty-five-foot motor cruiser, the property of Mrs. Faulkner, moored at the Ala Wai yacht basin. Mrs. Faulkner had insisted that they use it.

"Did you manage to get in touch with your daughter?" Nancy asked.

"Yes. She's waiting for you downtown." Mrs.

Faulkner gestured at the broad Victorian-style plantation house. "Nancy—Ned—why don't we let Bess and George enjoy their swim? We can talk up there."

She led them through the miniature rain forest that served as her garden. Tall feather palms cast cool shadows over brilliant displays of pink hibiscus and white gardenia.

Soon the three of them were seated in comfortable wicker chairs on the first-floor verandah. Resting her clasped hands on her knees, Nancy remarked, "Mrs. Faulkner, you said Lisa vanished on Friday."

"That's right. Friday afternoon. Diana phoned me as soon as she heard."

"It's Monday now. Why haven't you gone to the police yet?"

Alice looked around uncomfortably. "If it were up to me, I'd have the National Guard scouring the island. But my ex-son-in-law, Ross Rafferty, has forbidden it. He and Diana are Lisa's guardians." Her lip curled in disdain. "Ross wants the police kept out of it. You see, he's concerned about his reputation. I don't know why. He doesn't have much of one to protect."

"Mrs. Faulkner, you still could have gone to them. What's *your* reason for not contacting the police?"

A troubled look shadowed the old woman's

face. "The publicity would hurt my bank, Windward Fidelity. Windward Bancorp owns the bank. I have controlling interest in Windward Bancorp." Frowning, she leaned back in her chair and seemed to become lost in thought.

Nancy reached out and touched the woman's wrist gently. "Is that the real reason?"

Alice Faulkner shook her head slowly. Beneath Mrs. Faulkner's tough exterior, Nancy could see a tired old woman, worn down by her present problems. "Actually, I'm worried about Lisa, Nancy. I'm afraid I've made enemies in the business and banking community. Powerful enemies! They wouldn't hesitate to strike at me by harming my only grandchild."

How could they harm her if she ran away? Nancy thought. "Why are you so sure Lisa ran away then?"

"Diana never let me see much of my granddaughter." Alice's face filled with regret. "Like a fool, I stayed away. Still, I could see that Lisa wasn't happy. How could she be with all that turmoil in her life?" She shook her head sadly. "Apparently, Lisa had been planning this for quite a while."

"Why do you say that?"

"Because of the way she did it," Alice explained. "Diana was planning an art exhibit on Maui. She asked Lisa to stop at the bank to pick up her travelers' checks. You see, Diana kept extra checks along with her valuables in a safety deposit box at the bank."

Ned whistled in disbelief. "And the bank let her in? Just like that?"

Alice gave him a frosty look. "Young man, Lisa is a *Faulkner!* Windward *is* the family bank. Anyone in our family can enter the bank at any time and for any reason."

"What happened then?" Nancy asked.

"Once inside the safety deposit vault, Lisa grabbed her mother's diamonds and quite a few bearer bonds. Then she strolled out the door —and she hasn't been seen since!"

"And since anyone can cash in a bearer bond," Ned said, nodding, "Lisa will have enough money to do whatever she wants for a long time. How many bonds did she take?"

Alice sighed, her misery lining her troubled face. "Four hundred thousand dollars' worth! Her little surprise withdrawal wasn't discovered until closing time. When Lisa failed to return home, Diana called Ross at the bank. He checked the vault and very nearly had a heart attack! Diana phoned me immediately after that. Ross sent our security people to the airport, hoping to stop Lisa from leaving Hawaii. But Lisa never showed up."

Hawaii was a very difficult place to enter or leave, Nancy knew. Honolulu was the only international airport, and everyone had to pass through customs. Moreover, the North American mainland was more than two thousand miles to the east, beyond the range of most aircraft. Only a major airline could get Lisa to California.

So Lisa still had to be in Hawaii. There was no way the girl could convert those diamonds and bearer bonds to cash over the weekend. The process could take many days.

Nancy shivered suddenly. A teenage girl with four hundred grand in her purse was a walking target for every crook in the city!

Alice glanced at Nancy. "When you get to be my age, dear, the money doesn't seem that important anymore. *Family* is what really counts. I—I'm afraid I haven't been very lucky with mine." Taking a deep breath, she forced herself to go on. "My boys both died young. As for Diana—well, we haven't been close for many years. Since my husband's death, Diana has had very little to do with me. She's carved out a life for herself as an artist. After her divorce from Ross, she lived with Lisa in a condo on Kalakaua Avenue." The woman's haunted gaze traveled from Nancy to Ned. "I've made up my mind. I'm going to get custody of Lisa and start all over again." Tears glistened in her eyes. "I think I'll take Lisa back to Texas. Give her a good stable home for a change." Lower lip quivering, she blinked at Nancy. "Find my granddaughter, Nancy. Please. She's all I have left."

* * *

A short while later Nancy and her friends climbed into their rental car. Nancy settled comfortably behind the steering wheel and turned the key in the ignition. Then, swiveling the stick shift, she executed a perfect three-point turn and steered the tan sedan through the massive wrought-iron gates of the Faulkner estate.

"You know, I could really get used to this climate." Bess rolled down her rear window, letting the air wash over her. "I am going to be as brown as peanut butter when we get back to River Heights."

"I still can't get used to that estate," George said. "Has it been in the family long?"

"Since I hadn't spoken with the Faulkners recently, I did a little background reading on the family," Nancy replied, carefully guiding the car around a sharp turn. "Mrs. Faulkner's husband, C. K. Faulkner, was a self-made man and one of the richest people in the Islands. He left Mrs. Faulkner very well provided for. He bought the house and large pieces of oceanfront real estate all over the Islands."

"How big is this bank she mentioned?" asked Ned.

"Big!" Nancy whistled softly. "According to the magazine article I read, the bank's assets total nine hundred million dollars! Windward Fidelity is the biggest lender to all the countries of the Pacific Rim."

While she talked, Nancy kept her eyes straight

ahead. Tantalus Drive was a rattlesnake of a road, all winding curves and sudden downhill plunges. Luxurious estates, hidden by jungle growth, bordered the narrow road as it wound down into the city.

The car picked up speed as they descended an old lava ridge. The road swerved suddenly, heading straight for a jungle-covered hillside. Then it zigzagged again, carrying their car across a ridgeline that offered panoramic views of the Koolau Mountains and the sapphire-colored Pacific Ocean.

Nancy tightened her grip on the wheel. Tires squealed softly as they rounded a long bend, and Nancy's reddish gold hair whipped into her face. She pressed the brake again. The car slowed once more.

Ned touched her shoulder. "Better slow down, Nancy. We don't want to *fly* into Honolulu."

Nancy frowned as she studied the sheer basalt cliffs. "This road is one surprise after another. What did they do? Pave an old mule trail?"

Ned smiled. "I have confidence in your driving, Nancy."

Nancy had opened her mouth to reply when suddenly she no longer felt any pressure under her right foot. The brake pedal sank to the floor.

The sedan started down a long slope. Nancy felt the car shudder as it picked up speed. Frowning, she stomped on the brake pedal. Once, twice!

The pedal rested uselessly on the floor. Nancy's face turned white.

Ned clutched her shoulder. "Nancy, what's wrong?"

"Brace yourselves, guys!" Nancy watched in horror as the speedometer needle soared past fifty. "This car has just lost its brakes!"

Chapter

Two

TIRES SQUEALED IN protest as the car fishtailed around a long bend. Nancy could feel it lightly touching the road, a sure sign that it was about to spin out and roll over. The rear wheel skidded ominously toward the edge of the road.

Nancy cut the wheels to the left, then to the right. The car seesawed back and forth across the center line, but its tires held the asphalt. Wide-eyed with terror, Nancy watched the speedometer needle creep higher and higher.

Fifty-five—sixty—*sixty-five!*

Ahead, Tantalus Drive dissolved into a series of sweeping hairpin turns. Nancy's stomach felt as if it were falling down a well. The car was

10

traveling much too fast. Unless she could find a way to slow it down, they would go hurtling right off the side of the mountain!

She tried to pump the brakes again. Nothing! And the first hairpin turn was coming up fast.

Nancy's eyes flew desperately around the front seat. Then they zeroed in on the stick shift. I'll put the engine in another gear, she thought. That ought to cut our speed.

Nancy jammed the stick shift into low gear. Then, gripping the steering wheel even harder, she hollered, "Hang on!"

The sedan took the bend on two wheels, hugging the forested slope. But with the engine in a lower gear, the car began to slow down. The needle fell past sixty. The car felt heavier—more a part of the road.

On the next straightaway, Nancy swung the steering wheel from side to side. The sedan performed a lazy ballet, losing speed with each swerve. Nancy knocked the speed down to forty. But the next hairpin turn boosted it right back up to sixty again!

Nancy wanted to weep. They were still rolling too fast. At this speed, they were certain to jump the road on the next turn.

Suddenly Ned shouted, "Nancy, look!"

There was a grassy area on the right-hand side of the road, just before the bend.

"Nancy! The turnaround! Bank into it!" Ned cried.

Nancy spun the wheel all the way over. The car shuddered as it jumped the embankment. Gritting her teeth, Nancy held the wheel steady.

Screeeeeeech! The car performed a perfect loop, its tires chopping up the grass. Then Nancy yanked on the emergency brake, and the car shrieked to a halt, rocking on its springs. Its blunt nose was pointing back uphill.

Nancy exhaled heavily, resting her forehead on the steering wheel. She peered out the side window—and shuddered violently.

Just inches from the car's tires, the grassy area plunged abruptly into a misty valley. A long sea gull whizzed past, oblivious to the car perched above him.

Trembling in relief, Nancy whispered, "Everybody all right?"

Ned nodded. He stumbled out of the car, and Bess and George followed a moment later. Nancy waited until she was sure her legs would support her. Her knees felt as limp as cooked spaghetti.

Ned was studying the tire gouges in the turf. Looking back uphill, he remarked, "This is *not* a road to lose your brakes on. We're going to need a tow truck. We broke the axle when we spun around."

"Ned, would you stay with the car until the tow truck gets here?" Nancy asked. "I'll call a garage from the marina."

"You mean we've got to *walk* back to Ala Wai?" Bess protested. "Nancy, I don't know if I'm up to it. Not after that!"

"Well, we don't have to walk all the way." Nancy smiled reassuringly. "I noticed a bus stop at the bottom of Tantalus Drive."

"Let's go," George urged, turning her back on the wreck. "The less I see of that car, the better I'll feel."

George led the way downhill. Bess trudged along right behind. "And on top of everything else, it's so hot," she complained. "You're the one who likes hiking cross-country, George."

Nancy brought up the rear. She couldn't stop thinking about the accident. If a car's brakes were going to fail, Tantalus Drive wasn't the place for it to happen. Yet the car was last year's model. Had it been tampered with?

Nancy made up her mind to find out.

Nancy replaced the cordless phone in its bulkhead cradle. "We're all set," she told George. "The tow truck's on its way out. But the guy at the gas station said we have to go to the airport to fill out an accident report for the car rental company. Feel like taking a ride?"

"Love to."

Nancy crossed the *Kahala*'s teakwood cabin and peered into the aft stateroom. "How about you, Bess?"

"Not me!" Bess lay on the double bunk, her arm draped across her forehead. "Not after that hike. I thought Oahu was a *little* island!"

"Suit yourself." Nancy began to close the louvered hatch, then thought better of it. "Bess, after we're gone, make sure you lock the hatch, okay?"

Bess blinked in surprise. "Okay. But why?"

Nancy had made up her mind to ask the rental people a few pointed questions about that car. But there was no sense in getting Bess all worked up over what might turn out to be nothing.

"It's a good habit to get into. Don't mind me, I'm just a little jumpy today." Nancy closed the hatch. "We'll be back in a little while."

After taking a quick shower, Nancy retired to her cabin and put on a cream-colored sailing shirt and shorts. Then she and George hailed a cab to take them to the airport.

They found Sunrise Rentals in the main terminal, sandwiched in between the lockers and a fast-food restaurant. The Sunrise clerk was a slender young woman with large glasses who looked very shy. A name tag reading "Meredith" was pinned to her shirt.

She smiled as George and Nancy approached. "Hi! May I help you?"

"We're here to report an accident," Nancy said, slipping off her shoulder bag. "One of your cars. We rented it from another clerk—Janine —first thing this morning."

Meredith immediately reached for an official-looking document. Picking up a pen, she asked for Nancy's name and a description of the accident. Then she turned and studied the pigeonholes behind her. "One moment, please." She reached into a slot, withdrew a piece of paper, and stared at it for a long moment.

Facing the girls again, Meredith lowered her glasses. "That can't be right. We have *no car* rented to a Nancy Drew!"

Chapter

Three

W HAT!" NANCY EXCLAIMED, surprised. "I was here this morning. Janine made me sign for it. You people rented me that car."

Meredith showed her the front of the paper. "I'm sorry, but your name's not on the master list. You're not in our records."

"Wait a minute!" Nancy rummaged in her shoulder bag. "I've got the rental agreement right here." She put it on the counter. "Janine gave me this when I arrived. While she typed it up, she had me sign your master roster and list everyone in my party. Then she gave me this agreement and the car keys, and I left."

Looking a bit confused, Meredith glanced at

16

the shelf again. "Hmmmm. Maybe Janine misfiled it."

Nancy waited patiently while the girl carefully examined the rental agreement. All at once, Meredith's face brightened with understanding. "Ah, now I see." She put down the agreement. "We were booked solid yesterday. I talked to your credit card company—told them we had no cars available. Didn't they get in touch with you?"

Nancy sighed. "If they tried, we were probably already airborne. "But if my request didn't go through, why was this car waiting for me when I arrived?"

"Someone else rented the car for you." Meredith pointed out a block of print. "See? 'Hold for Nancy Drew and party.' Just before we closed yesterday, a woman called and said she wanted to rent a car for you."

"A woman?" George said. "Mrs. Faulkner?"

"She didn't identify herself," Meredith answered. "She said she was from the Malihini Corporation and asked for one of the corporate cars we keep on standby. She even named the car—tan four-door sedan, license number HI-9876."

"Corporate cars?" echoed Nancy. "What do you mean?"

"We keep a number of cars set aside for use by companies here in Honolulu," Meredith explained. "These companies have long-term rental agreements with us. Whenever they need a rental car in a hurry, we send one right over."

"Do you own these cars?" Nancy asked.

"Oh, no. We lease them on a six-month basis from car dealerships here in the Islands," Meredith replied.

Nancy frowned thoughtfully. "This Malihini Corporation—have you done business with them for very long?"

Meredith shook her head. "No. As a matter of fact, they're brand-new clients. I processed their agreement just the other day."

Just then, the airport intercom blared, "Nancy Drew, please report to the courtesy desk. You have a phone call."

Excusing herself, Nancy hurried across the lobby. At the paneled courtesy desk, a clerk handed Nancy a telephone.

"Hi, Nancy." It was Ned, and he sounded weary. "Bess told me you were at the airport. I'm down here at Kamaaina's gas station. We just finished putting that car on the lift."

"Is it in bad shape?"

"It was in bad shape when you rented it, Nancy. The brake drums are as bald as an eagle!" Anger sharpened his voice as he told her what else was wrong with it. "You want me to come down to the airport?"

"Stay where you are, Ned. We'll pick you up in a little while."

"Good enough. See you later."

After handing back the phone, Nancy returned to the Sunrise desk. "Meredith, you said the Malihini Corporation *specifically* requested that car for me?"

"Yes, they did."

Replacing the rental agreement in her bag, Nancy asked, "Where did that particular car come from?"

"We leased it from Smiling Al's Auto Sales in Pearl City." Meredith adjusted her glasses. "He sent it over first thing this morning."

Nancy took a pen from her shoulder bag. "Could you get me Smiling Al's address?"

"Certainly."

Meredith copied the address from the central file and handed it to Nancy. In another instant, Nancy and George were hurrying out to the taxi stand.

"Where are we going now?" George asked.

"First we pick up Ned," Nancy replied, opening the rear door of a cab. *"Then* we're going to see a man about a car. Ned says it was a rolling death trap." Nancy sat down and slammed the door shut. "I want to know *why* it was waiting for us when we arrived at the airport."

Smiling Al's Auto Sales wasn't hard to find. Its three-story cartoon billboard loomed huge above the Punanai Hills.

One of the showroom salesmen conducted them to the manager's office. A short, jowly man with bushy eyebrows and a receding hairline sat behind a sprawling mahogany desk. He had more diplomas on his wall than a doctor.

He looked up with a broad salesman's smile as Nancy and her friends entered. "Hi, I'm Al Lutsen. Smiling Al. What can I do for you?"

"I had a problem with one of your cars, Mr. Lutsen," Nancy said. "The brakes failed!"

"What car?" Al's smile vanished instantly. "When did this happen?"

"About two o'clock this afternoon," Nancy replied. "It was a tan four-door sedan. Remember it?"

"Vaguely." But Al's face gave him away. Nancy could tell that he remembered the car quite well. "What was wrong with it?"

Ned counted off points on his fingers. "One, the brake drums were bald. Two, the axle had rusted out. Three, the muffler fell off while it was on the lift—"

"I didn't sell you that car," Al blustered. "Why are you so interested?"

"You leased it to Sunrise Rentals this morning," Nancy replied. "They rented it to us. We were nearly killed in that clunker. So we're here for some answers, Mr. Lutsen."

Al cleared his throat and began shuffling through some papers. "Well, if you rented it from Sunrise, you'll have to take it up with them. I'm not responsible for cars once they leave the lot. I'm a busy man. Lot of work to do. Goodbye. Please close the door on your way out."

Ned leaned across the desk. "We're not leaving until we get our answers."

"I don't discuss the firm's business with outsiders."

Nancy cocked her head to one side. "Would you like to know where we're going next?" she asked.

Al's eyebrows lifted. "Where?"

"The Department of Transportation!" Nancy rested her fingertips on his desk. "I think they'll be very interested to hear that Smiling Al is putting unsafe cars on the road."

As the three turned to leave, Al jumped out of his chair and beat them to the door. "Whoa-whoa-whoa! Wait a minute! Let's talk about this, eh?" His salesman's smile had magically reappeared.

"How'd you come by that car?" Nancy asked.

Al shrugged. "I picked it up a couple of days ago. Got it from the Malihini Corporation."

Nancy's eyes widened. She glanced at George, who mirrored her look of astonishment. Al bit his lower lip. "Um, I said something?"

An excited note in her voice, Nancy asked, "How did this Malihini Corporation get in touch with you?"

"That's the funny part," Al recalled. "They sent me a telegram. 'Dear Mr. Lutsen.' I thought they were hitting me up for a donation at first. It was a little strange, but what a deal!"

"What do you mean, 'strange'?" Ned interjected.

"Well, the Malihini Corporation offered to sell me that car, but only if I leased it immediately to Sunrise Rentals," Al replied. "I had to scramble to do that. But it was worth it. The Malihini Corporation sold me that car for half the book value!"

Nancy scowled. "Why didn't your mechanics check out the car before you leased it to Sunrise?"

"I—I—I didn't have time for that," Al said lamely. "I had to have that car on the Sunrise lot first thing this morning. That was the deal. Hey, I couldn't pass that up. Half price? No way!" He stared uncomfortably at the trio. "Look, it was legitimate business. If you've got a beef about those brakes, you should talk to Sunrise."

"But it wasn't legitimate," Ned said. "You bought a clunker sight unseen and then dumped it on a rental agency. Pretty sloppy for a sharp businessman like yourself."

Nancy stepped forward. "Tell me more about the Malihini Corporation. Who are they? Have you ever done business with them before?"

"With them? Nahhhh! But I pick up old cars from companies all the time . . ." Meekly he sank into his chair. "Uh, maybe I could make it up to you, eh?"

22

"Yes, you could," George fumed. "Why don't you test-drive that car?"

"Now, there's no need to get nasty." Al's smile resurrected itself. "I understand your situation. You're in Hawaii, and you don't have a car for sight-seeing. But, listen, I'm always willing to help. Why, I'd be delighted to rent you lovely ladies—and you, sir—a brand-new car right out of the showroom for as long as you're in the Islands."

"No charge!" added Nancy grimly.

Al scratched the back of his head. He showed Nancy a sidelong frown. "Ah—couldn't we negotiate something about mileage?"

An hour later in a new car provided by Smiling Al, Nancy drove her friends back to Honolulu. She steered the car down the Kamehameha Highway, keeping an eye on the rush-hour traffic.

Nancy's thoughts were racing. The Malihini Corporation had originally owned that damaged car. They had sold it to Smiling Al at a price he couldn't resist—but only on the condition that he lease it immediately to Sunrise Rentals. Next, the Malihini Corporation had called Sunrise and arranged to have that particular car waiting for Nancy Drew.

Ned gave her a long look. "You're awfully quiet."

"I'm thinking about that nice little booby trap the Malihini Corporation left for us," Nancy

23

replied as she steered the car down the exit. "Whoever they are, they went to a lot of trouble to cover their tracks. They knew we were going to visit Alice Faulkner. They knew we would be coming down Tantalus Drive on the way home. You can guess the rest."

"You bet," Ned replied. "Our crash would have looked like a simple accident. No one would have traced it all the way back to the Malihini Corporation."

"Nancy, what do you make of all this?" George asked.

"I don't know, George." Sighing, Nancy turned the car into the Ala Wai parking lot. "None of it makes sense. What is this Malihini Corporation? Why did they try to kill us the moment we arrived in Honolulu?" She eased the car into a parking space. "Ned, George—we'd better be very, very careful from now on, okay?"

Ned nodded in agreement. "I'll go along with that."

After grabbing their gear, the trio headed down the floating walkway that connected the individual berths. Sunset painted the sea a vivid bronze. Fat gulls rested on barnacle-encrusted piles and watched the boat owners close up for the night.

The *Kahala* lolled at her berth. Her fiberglass hull made thudding noises as it jostled the pier. George sighed. "Am I glad to be home. Know something? I haven't had a bite to eat all day."

"Why don't you and Bess make sandwiches?" Nancy suggested. "That'll give me a chance to phone Mrs. Faulkner's daughter."

Just then, Bess appeared at the *Kahala*'s fantail, smiling and waving a greeting. All at once a look of horror flashed across her face.

"Nancy! Behind you! *Look out!*"

Nancy turned just in time to see a sailboat's boom swinging toward them. The thick wooden beam was hurtling straight at her face!

Chapter

Four

Nancy grabbed her friends and threw herself forward. The sail struck her high on the shoulder, but the boom sailed harmlessly past.

Nancy, Ned, and George hit the walkway together. The impact drove water through the slats, soaking the trio to the skin.

"Oh!" a woman cried out. "Are you kids all right?"

"Nobody was hurt." Getting up, Nancy saw a plump woman standing on the deck of a moored Catalina whose boom was suspended over the walkway.

"Talk about 'low bridge'!" George exclaimed, standing up.

"I'm awfully sorry," the woman said. "I thought that winch was locked. It started unwinding the minute I turned my back. I never meant to—"

"That's okay. No harm done." Nancy smiled reassuringly.

Nancy and her friends pushed the boom back aboard the woman's boat. Then they joined Bess at the *Kahala*. After assuring Bess that they were all right, they boarded the cruiser.

While Ned and George were changing clothes, Nancy used the boat's cordless phone to call Lisa's mother. The phone at the other end rang three times. Then a woman's voice answered. "Hello?"

"Mrs. Rafferty, this is Nancy Drew—"

"Nancy Drew!" the woman interrupted. "Where have you people been? Mother said you were coming hours ago."

"Our rental car broke down. We were delayed reporting the accident. I am sorry," Nancy said apologetically. "Listen, I can be there in half an hour."

"All right. Come right over."

"See you then." Nancy hung up. "Bess, you and George stay here and cover the phone in case Mrs. Faulkner tries to reach us. We'll be back soon."

"Okay." Bess put a couple of sandwiches and two cans of soda in a plastic bag, then handed the bundle to Nancy. "Good luck."

Grinning, Ned opened the hatch. "We may need it."

Diana Rafferty's apartment was two miles east of the marina, in an ultramodern building. Nancy parked in the beach lot opposite it. Then dodging the traffic, she and Ned dashed across the street.

Nancy pressed the doorbell at an upper-floor apartment. The door swung open to reveal a slender, tight-lipped woman with a soft blond ponytail and Alice Faulkner's blue eyes.

Diana blinked in surprise. "Nancy Drew?"

"That's me." Nancy offered a pleasant smile. "And this is my friend Ned Nickerson."

"Excuse me, it's just—" Flustered, Diana opened the door all the way. "Well—you're a *kid.*"

"Eighteen, Mrs. Rafferty," Nancy replied, holding her smile in place. Alice Faulkner's polished manners hadn't rubbed off on her daughter.

"I hope my mother knows what she's doing." Diana led the way into her living room. "Please. Make yourselves comfortable. Oh, I really should mention that I don't like to be called that name. I prefer 'Diana Faulkner.'"

Nancy nodded politely and sat down. Her gaze wandered around the room, taking in the large windows, modern furniture, and tropical plants. Diana's paintings hung in prominent places along the walls, each one emblazoned with her signature. The paintings were all nature studies —flaming volcanoes, ferocious blue seas, stormy landscapes.

"The last time you saw Lisa was Friday morning, wasn't it?" Nancy asked.

"Yes." Diana gave a dramatic sigh. "When she left for school." Her voice quavered. "I—I just don't understand why she did it—why she ran away. I mean, if she had a problem, she could have come to me. Right? I'm her *mother*."

Toying with an earring, Diana added, "I suppose I ought to be grateful for your help. Do you think you can find her?"

"The more you tell me, the better our chances." Nancy settled back in her chair. "Why did you send Lisa to the bank that day?"

"I needed my travelers' checks. I was planning to be gone a few days. An exhibit of my work." Her lips tightened. "You see, despite the opposition of my mother and my ex-husbands—all four of them!—I've made quite a name for myself as an artist. That's why this business irritates me no end!"

Puzzled, Nancy asked, "What do you mean?"

"I had to miss my opening because of this mess. I'm supposed to be on Maui, not sitting around here trying to figure out what got into Lisa!"

Diana's self-centeredness took Nancy's breath

29

away. With Lisa missing, how could Diana even think about an art exhibit?

"Why didn't you go to the bank yourself?" Nancy prodded.

"There was a strike at the hotel I was booked into. I had to make other arrangements."

"Did Lisa do this sort of thing for you often?"

"Now and then. I tried to get her to be more helpful around here. She was so sullen at times. As if she held me personally responsible for all the trouble in her life. Trouble! That girl doesn't know the meaning of the word!"

"She does now," Ned observed quietly.

Ignoring his comment, Diana scowled and snapped, "How could Lisa do it? How? If word of this ever gets out, I'll be the laughingstock of Honolulu!"

No wonder poor Lisa ran away! Nancy thought.

"Can you tell me something about Lisa's friends?" she asked, resting her chin on her fist.

"Not much. There was a girl who was always hanging around here—Dawn something. I forget her last name. I met her only once or twice." Diana pushed her dainty glasses up on her nose. "I happen to be a very busy woman. Most people think artists work when they feel the urge. Not so! When I prepare for an exhibit, I have to do ten or twelve canvases." Closing her eyes, she stroked her forehead gingerly. "I—I can't understand it. I just can't! Lisa knew how important that exhibit is. How could she *do* this to me now?"

Stifling a surge of irritation, Nancy stood up and exhaled slowly. "Ms. Faulkner, could I look at Lisa's bedroom?"

"Go ahead. It's upstairs. Second door on the right."

"Thanks. I'll be right back. Ned, maybe you could get directions to Lisa's school from Ms. Faulkner. We'll definitely want to visit there."

Nancy climbed the carpeted stairs and slipped into the darkened room. She flicked on the light, noting the cedarwood bureau and sound system and home computer. On the bed, a teddy bear forlornly awaited his owner's return.

There was a personalized notepad on the ink-stained blotter on Lisa's desk. Picking it up, Nancy tilted the top sheet toward the light. Faint impressions were visible. If she could enhance them, there might be a clue here.

Nancy took a lead pencil and lightly colored across the paper. Only a few impressions came through in the sheen of gray. The upper left corner showed the clearest markings:

Miss Mi
1276 Pr
San Fra

An address, Nancy realized. Miss Mi? Who could that be? Perhaps a friend of Lisa's.

Peeling the paper from the pad, Nancy folded it and tucked it into her shoulder bag. Just then, a hanging object drew her gaze. It was a model helicopter, an army Huey, suspended from a nylon thread.

All in all, the rest of Lisa's room seemed pretty normal for a sixteen-year-old girl. But that model helicopter didn't fit. Nancy studied it for a long moment, then shrugged.

Next she picked up a photo cube on the bureau. All six photos were of a lovely girl with brownish blond hair and striking blue eyes. Three of the pictures showed Lisa alone. One pictured her with a cute dark-haired girl —another with a grinning strawberry blonde. The final snapshot showed all three girls at an airport, hamming it up in front of a Huey helicopter.

Looks as though Lisa is interested in flying, Nancy thought, glancing back at the model. I wonder if her mother knows how much?

Nancy felt a twinge of sadness. Since her mother's death, Carson Drew had tried to be both a mother and a father to her. What would my life have been like if Dad had been like Diana Faulkner? she wondered. If he had been too wrapped up in himself to care about me?

Dismissing that depressing thought, Nancy stood at the corner of the window and peered through the venetian blinds. Across the street, black feather palms waved languidly in the night breeze.

And then Nancy saw him.

He was a dark-skinned, broad-shouldered man in a Hawaiian shirt. Moon face and slicked-back hair. Nervously tapping his toe on the sidewalk, he was leaning against a streetlight, arms folded —his gaze never leaving Lisa Trumbull's window.

Who was he? And why was he spying on Lisa's bedroom?

"Ned! Get up here—quick!" she called.

Footsteps sounded on the stairs. Ned burst through the doorway with Diana right behind.

"Somebody on the sidewalk is watching this window," Nancy whispered.

Ned circled the window and came up on Nancy's side. Easing a slat upward, he glanced at the street. Then he looked at Nancy. "You're right."

"Who?" Diana rushed to the window.

Nancy tried to stop her. *"Don't!* He'll see you—"

Too late! Diana's outline broke the shaft of light. Glancing at the street, Nancy saw the moon-faced man flinch. He averted his face at once and turned away, heading for the nightclub district with a hasty stride.

No doubt about it. He was spying on Lisa's bedroom. And now he was getting away!

Chapter

Five

"COME ON, NED!"

Nancy dashed out of the bedroom and down the stairs. She reached the front door in thirty seconds, yanked it open, and rushed onto the outdoor balcony.

She just caught a glimpse of the man's Hawaiian shirt in the park across the street. Then a bus hissed to a stop at the curb. The dark-haired man jumped aboard. With a throaty rumble, the bus lumbered away. She'd lost him!

Ned came up behind her. "Great try, Nancy. We would've had him if we'd been on the first floor."

They turned and headed back into the apartment. Diana was waiting at the door, her face tense. "Who was that man?" she asked.

"We were hoping you could tell us," Nancy replied.

"I haven't any idea. I've never seen anyone hanging around in front of our building. Do you think he had something to do with Lisa's running away?"

"He may have. But I'll tell you one thing, Ms. Faulkner." Nancy tilted her head toward the window. "If that man or anyone had anything to do with Lisa's disappearance, then your daughter may be in a lot of trouble. I'd think long and hard about calling the police. I'd think *really* hard."

Diana swallowed hard. "Wha—what are we going to do?"

"We're going to find Lisa," Nancy said simply. She asked for permission to borrow the photo cube. Diana consented readily, and Ned hurried upstairs to fetch it.

Diana sat down slowly, her head bowed. Tears collected in the lower rims of her eyes. "I—I tried my best." She began to sob. "I did! We just c-could n-never talk to each other. Please try to understand that."

Nancy touched the woman's shoulder as Ned arrived with the photo cube. Without a word, Nancy tilted her chin toward the door. She and Ned left quietly, and she closed the door gingerly behind her.

"What do we do now?" asked Ned, escorting her back to the parking lot.

"Go to Lisa's school first thing tomorrow and find out who her friends are. We'll talk to them." Nancy opened her car door. "Maybe they can tell us where she might have gone."

Ned dropped into the passenger seat. "You look pretty grim, Nancy. What is it?"

"I'm feeling pretty grim." Nancy turned the ignition key. "I don't like the way this is shaping up, Ned. Mrs. Faulkner hires me to find her missing granddaughter. A company I never heard of tries to kill us. An unknown man has Lisa's home under surveillance. What's the connection?"

Ned shrugged. "You've got me."

"It's not what we know," Nancy replied, shifting into reverse. "It's what we *don't* know! And in a case like this, what we don't know can get us all killed!"

Promptly at eight the next morning Nancy drove into the parking lot of Roosevelt High School. Bright sunshine dappled the huge lawn and isolated coconut palms of the campus.

Bess stepped out of the car, turning her face toward the sun. "Glorious!" she said. "If I lived in Honolulu, I'd have the worst attendance record in school."

Nancy smiled and pulled on the brake. Earlier that morning Bess and George had volunteered to go undercover at the school, to try to learn more about Lisa. Ned had offered to talk to the custodians.

"First stop for me is the principal's office," Bess announced. "I'll pretend to be a transfer student. Maybe I can get a look at Lisa's file."

"I'm going to the guidance office," George said.

Ned grinned. "It's the boiler room for me."

Nancy stepped out of the car. "Okay, we've all got investigating to do. Let's meet back here at ten-thirty. Good hunting."

The first bell jangled as Nancy was crossing the campus. Kids in jeans and button-down shirts ambled into the cinderblock building, jostling and laughing with one another. Threading her way through the crowd, Nancy headed down the hall.

Although she had Lisa's photo, Nancy was reluctant to show it around. The minute she did, she'd be marked as an outsider. So she drifted from group to group—introducing herself as a transfer student, seeking out the class gossips, dropping a question here and there.

By the time the homeroom bell rang, Nancy had learned a number of things about RHS. Karen Rothenberg was running for junior class president. Super-hunk Troy Shepherd had broken up with Marcia Kirtland. And Lisa Trumbull's best friend was named Dawn Burnham.

A girl pointed out Dawn's homeroom. Nancy

took up a position by the door. Ten minutes later, the electric bell cut loose with an earsplitting clang and kids streamed into the hallway. Nancy spotted Dawn at once.

"Hi, Dawn! Wait up a minute, will you?" Nancy followed behind her.

Dawn halted and turned, an inquiring expression on her face. Nancy answered the unspoken question. "I'm Nancy Drew. I just transferred in."

Dawn smiled uncertainly. "Maybe I've seen you around."

Nancy fell into step beside the girl. "I was wondering if you and Lisa Trumbull could help me."

"Depends." Dawn shrugged, hugging her books close.

"My dad's in the navy. Just got transferred to Pearl," Nancy said smoothly. "When we lived in Florida, I was in a flying club. I want to join one here."

Dawn's eyes lit up. "You're into flying? Fixed or rotary wing?"

"Rotary." Nancy was suddenly glad that Ned had talked her into learning to fly a couple of years ago.

"Oh, boy! Lisa is sure going to want to meet you." Dawn grinned as the two of them hurried along. "Lisa and I belong to a flying club in Wailuha. Lisa's way ahead of me, though. She's got her pilot's license and instrument rating, and

38

she's about ten hours away from getting her rotary-wing ticket. Lisa loves choppers. Last summer, at camp in California, she went up in a Huey, and it was love at first sight."

"She went to flight school in California?"

"No, just summer camp. Picasso sent her to a ranch near Bishop."

"Picasso?"

"Lisa's mom. Di the Artist. Usually, Lisa hated being sent away like that. But this gave her a chance to be with Michele again."

"Michele?" Nancy prodded.

"Yeah. Michele Woodbridge." Dawn's sigh was nostalgic. "Me, Lisa, and Michele used to hang out together in junior high. We were real close, all three of us. Then Michele's parents got a divorce, and she moved to San Francisco with her mom." A sad look came over Dawn's face. "By that point, things were getting pretty nasty for Lisa at home, too. Her mother's latest marriage was breaking up. Lisa told me her mother and that Rafferty guy used to fight like cats and dogs. Flying kitchenware and everything!" Dawn shook her head. "Boy, when I think back, it sure wasn't easy for Lisa. Di used to fight with all of her husbands. When we were little, Lisa practically lived at Michele's house—"

Brrrinnnnng! The late bell jangled mercilessly. Dawn cast a worried look at her classroom. There was time for only one more question.

"San Francisco? You guys must really miss Michele. Do you stay in touch?"

"Lisa does. She writes once a week. Me, I'm no writer. Listen, Nancy, I've got to go. See you at lunch?"

"One of these days. Take care, Dawn."

Doing a brisk about-face, Nancy headed up the corridor. Ned and Bess met her halfway. "Did you learn anything?" Ned asked.

"A little. I think now I understand why Lisa ran away." Nancy turned to Bess. "How'd you make out?"

"Not so well. I got into the central filing system, but all I found was Lisa's locker number —four-forty-seven," Bess replied.

"How'd you manage that?" asked Ned.

"Easy. I told the main secretary I was a transfer student. She asked me for my transcript, and I told her it was back home in North Dakota. When she went into the principal's office to make the call privately, I sneaked a peek."

"North Dakota?" Nancy echoed.

"Yeah, I told her I was Bess Summers from Grand Forks, North Dakota. I figured that would keep her on the phone for a while," Bess added proudly.

Nancy cleared her throat. "Bess, did you stop to think what will happen when she calls Grand Forks and finds out Bess Summers doesn't exist?"

Just then, the overhead intercom blared, "Bess

40

Summers, report to the front office. Bess Summers, report to the office *immediately!*"

"Better go hide in the car," Nancy suggested. "Your cover is blown!"

Ned hurried down the hall. "I'll go look for George."

"Good idea. I'll be along in a few minutes." Nancy took off in the opposite direction. She had something she wanted to try.

Nancy found Lisa's locker in the science section. Kneeling, she put her ear to the steel. Her fingers turned the dial to the left. A musical *ting!* sounded. Taking a deep breath, she reversed the turn ever so slowly. Once, twice around the dial, then—*ting!* She wiped her sweating fingers on her pants leg, then painstakingly moved the dial to the left again. *Ting!*

Nancy stood up and gave the handle a quick tug. The door swung open. Immediately Nancy noticed a colorful bit of paper on the top shelf. She pulled it free. It was an airline brochure, a schedule of flights and departure times. One line was circled in ink.

FLIGHT 227   HNL-SFC   2:30 P.M.

Familiar with airline codes, Nancy knew that HNL-SFC stood for "Honolulu to San Francisco." She grinned excitedly. It was all coming together now. She pulled out the note she had taken from Lisa's bedroom.

41

Miss Mi
1276 Pr
San Fra

Now it's clear, Nancy thought. *Mi* stands for *Michele*. Michele Woodbridge. And Michele lives in *San Francisco*.

Now Nancy understood how Lisa had pulled it off. Lisa had been angry when she wrote to Michele. Perhaps she had hinted at leaving home for good. Perhaps Michele had offered her a place to stay. Lisa's big problem had been getting the airfare to fly out of Honolulu. And Diana had solved that problem when she had sent Lisa to the bank. Only Lisa had never made it to the airport. She was still out there. . . .

Suddenly a brawny hand closed around Nancy's wrist. She gasped.

"What are you doing here?" a man's voice growled in her ear.

Chapter

Six

Turning, Nancy looked into a rugged face. The man was big and broad-shouldered. He looked like a boxer with more losses than wins. Beside him stood a tall, goateed black man. They were both too old for high school.

"I asked you a question," the first man muttered. His grip tightened on Nancy's wrist.

Nancy's heart thudded against her rib cage as the man backed her up against the locker.

At that moment a teacher stepped out of the biology lab and came forward, her face stern. "Gentlemen, I'll have to ask you to leave. If you don't stop bothering that girl, I'll call the police!"

The white man sighed. He reached into his

blazer, produced a wallet, and flipped it open. A silver badge gleamed. "We *are* the police."

"We'll handle things from here on in, ma'am," the black man said, leading Nancy away. He clucked his tongue in reproof. "Breaking into other people's lockers? Young lady, it looks as though you've got some detention time ahead of you."

"Wait a minute!" Nancy said. "I'm not a student here. My name is Nancy Drew. I'm a private investigator from the mainland. I'm trying to find Lisa Trumbull. She's run away."

"A PI, eh?" the white cop remarked. "And I suppose you don't know that all private eyes must register with the local police department before they go to work here in the Islands."

"I'm not a licensed investigator," Nancy explained. "I sort of help people out when they're in trouble."

"I think I've heard of you." The black cop studied Nancy with a new respect. "You cracked that airlines case in Seattle, didn't you?"

"That's right," Nancy said.

"Then it's a pleasure to meet you, Nancy." The first cop offered his hand. "I'm Tim Di-Prizio, detective-sergeant, Honolulu P.D. This is my partner, Detective-Sergeant Martin Giles."

Martin took out his notebook. "What's this about Lisa Trumbull?"

"Aren't you two here to investigate Lisa's

running away? I thought her mother had decided to call you."

"This is the first I've heard of it," Martin said.

Nancy hastily explained how she had been called into the case. When she had finished, she asked, "Why were you guys watching Lisa's locker?"

"Marty and I are on street detail this week," Tim DiPrizio explained. "We patrol the malls —keep an eye out for con artists. This morning, one of our informers told us that something big is going down. There's a girl on the street—Lisa Trumbull—with something very valuable to sell. The word is, she's got diamonds."

"The name didn't ring any bells with us," Martin added. "So we decided to check the high school. We staked out the girl's locker. Figured to ask her a few questions when she showed up."

Nancy was really worried now. Cops never heard anything first. If the word had gotten to them, then every street person in Honolulu must know that Lisa Trumbull was carrying something worth big bucks. Lisa was in more danger than ever before.

"Look, maybe we can help each other," Nancy suggested. "You guys know the street scene. You can tell me where Lisa might try to sell those diamonds. In return, I'll tell you what I know."

"Sounds good to me," Tim said. "Where do you think Lisa's headed?"

"San Francisco. She has a friend there named Michele Woodbridge."

"We'll check it out." Martin turned to his partner. "Hey, Tim, if you were a high schooler looking to unload merchandise, who would you go to?"

Tim snapped his fingers. "Boomer! He's a fence—you know, he buys stolen goods," he replied. "Boomer hangs out at the Ala Moana shopping center. Big, beefy guy in his early twenties." They described him further. "Someone's bound to steer Lisa to him."

Nancy smiled grimly. "I think I'll have a talk with this guy."

"No way," Tim warned. "You'll never get near him. We've sent our best undercover people after him. Boomer has a sixth sense about cops. And he can run like a jackrabbit."

"But I'm not a cop," Nancy replied, heading for the exit. "Thanks for the help, guys. I'll be in touch."

A short while later Nancy, Ned, and Bess stood in the middle of the Ala Moana mall. "Bess, I need your shopping expertise." Nancy steered her friend toward a classy boutique. "Go in there and get me some earrings and bracelets."

"Hey, that's easy!" Bess giggled and hurried into the store.

Nancy and Ned waited beside the tall fountains in the center of the mall.

"I wonder how George is doing at the bank," Nancy remarked.

Ned shrugged. "I hope she's getting more out of Mr. Rafferty than we got out of Lisa's mother."

Bess rejoined them a half hour later, proudly displaying a pair of gold earrings and a trio of shiny bracelets. Nancy examined each one carefully and tucked them in the pockets of her jeans.

"You guys go watch the exits," she suggested. "I'll stay here. Flash me a signal if you see anyone who matches Boomer's description."

Ned and Bess sauntered off to their respective sentry posts. Nancy seated herself on a lava wall and settled down to wait.

Two hours passed. Nancy breathed deeply, forcing herself to stay alert. Sooner or later, their quarry would show.

Nancy's gaze drifted toward Ned. She sat up straight. Ned was vigorously scratching his ear!

Anxiously she gazed through the crowd. And then she saw him. Boomer was taller than she'd expected, with bushy hair. Ultra-dark sunglasses concealed his eyes. He walked like a lion on the prowl.

Nancy strolled up beside him. "Hi, Boomer!" She dug into her pocket, then displayed the earrings in her upturned palm. "What do you think of them?"

Picking up an earring, he studied it carefully. "Expensive."

47

Nancy grinned slyly. "Not when you've got a five-finger discount."

"My favorite kind!" Boomer laughed, then stared at Nancy with mock severity. "You? A shoplifter? Shame on you!"

"Only when I need the money." Nancy pretended to look around nervously. "How much can I get for this stuff?"

Boomer stared at her for a long moment. Finally he tossed the earring into her outstretched palm. Walking past her, he whispered, "Parking garage. Ten minutes."

Nancy breathed deeply, then coughed, as the strong gasoline fumes of the Ala Moana garage filled her lungs. She was perched on her car's front fender. Casting a glance to the right, she saw Ned loitering at the up-ramp. Just knowing he was there made her feel better.

Then Boomer came down the steel stairway from the mall, boot heels hammering the metal. Looking around suspiciously, he went straight to Nancy's car.

"Here's how we work it," Boomer muttered. "You get half now. Then you take your stuff upstairs, go to the public phone, and leave it in the coin return. The rest of your money'll be in there."

"How much?" asked Nancy.

"Thirty bucks."

"In the coin return? Anyone could take it!"

Boomer grinned evilly. "It's being watched. No one will—"

He halted abruptly. Face frozen, he stared at a reflection in the neighboring car's windshield. Nancy heard a footstep behind her.

Glancing over her shoulder, she gasped out loud. Approaching the stairs was the moon-faced man—the same man who had been spying on Lisa Trumbull's apartment!

Boomer seemed to sense Nancy's anxiety. "Be cool. He's not going to bust us."

"You know him?" Nancy blurted.

"Nahhhh, but he's a cop." Boomer leaned casually against the other car. "I can tell. That joker's got *plainclothes* written all over him."

Nancy sneaked a quick glance. The moon-faced man lingered at the bottom of the stairs. Then, pretending not to look at them, he ambled over to the *Star-Bulletin* dispenser and bought a newspaper.

Alarmed, Nancy realized that he was shadowing her!

Nancy's heartbeat seemed to fill her chest. The moon-faced man stood blocking the stairs, pretending to read his paper.

Nancy turned and noticed Boomer's suspicious gaze. He was glowering at her. His expression grew more menacing as he realized he couldn't escape up the stairs.

Suddenly his hand darted inside his leather jacket. "Now I get it! He's with *you!*" A small

49

pistol appeared in his big hand. "You set me up, you little—You're a *cop!*"

Before Nancy could move, Boomer had looped his arm around her neck. He held her in a choke-hold, using her as a shield as his pistol swiveled toward the moon-faced man. "Game's over, cop! Back off, you hear me?"

Nancy felt the cold steel of the gun against her temple.

"Back off, I said, or this is the end of her!"

Chapter

Seven

THIS IS IT, cop!" Boomer tapped the muzzle against Nancy's head. "Say goodbye to your partner."

Mouth agape, the moon-faced man stared at them. He held out a quaking hand. "N-now wait a minute, buddy! You got it all wrong!"

"You're following me!" Boomer roared, his left arm locked under Nancy's chin. "Lousy, stinking cop!"

Uttering a frightened yelp, the man turned and fled.

Boomer leveled the pistol and took careful aim at the man.

Now! Nancy thought.

Her head whipped back, striking Boomer flush on the chin. He yowled. Feeling his grip loosen, Nancy slipped out from under and gave him a solid judo chop to the ribs. Boomer stumbled. Nancy jumped him, grabbing his wrist with both hands, and hammered his gun hand against the fender. The pistol clattered to the floor. Nancy's foot swept it under a nearby car.

She heard running feet—the anxious shouts of Ned and Bess.

Boomer bolted. "More cops!"

After he ran up to Nancy, Ned hugged her. "You all right?"

"I'm fine." She pointed at Boomer, who was heading for the stairwell. "After him, Ned! We can't let him get away."

Ned and Nancy took off in pursuit. Bess brought up the rear. They charged up the stairway in single file, Ned in the lead. Nancy took the steps two at a time. She was thinking, What was that moon-faced guy doing here? Was he following me? But how does he know who I am? He couldn't have seen me in Lisa's window!

Clang! Boomer pushed a steel trash can over the edge of the stairs. It tumbled toward them!

Ned tried to dodge, but his foot slipped on the step. The can rolled right over him, and he went down hard.

"Ned!" Grabbing Bess, Nancy pushed her against the railing. The can bounced past them, spilling trash all over the stairs.

"I'm okay, Nancy. Go get him!" Ned said.

Nancy raced to the balcony. She spotted Boomer's blue- and orange-flowered shirt just ahead, disappearing into the mall crowd.

Shoving people aside, Boomer bulled his way down the main corridor. Angry shouts exploded all around him. Nancy stayed on his heels, zig-zagging between startled shoppers.

At last the crowd thinned out and disappeared. They were in a little turnoff now, a hallway lined with supply closets. Once in the clear, Nancy put on a sudden burst of speed. She came right up behind Boomer and brought him down with a tackle worthy of a pro football player.

Nancy and Boomer rolled over and over across the polished floor. Breaking free, Nancy jumped to her feet. Boomer got up groggily, saw who it was, and—snarling with rage—threw himself at Nancy.

Nancy's right leg scissored in a flawless judo kick. Her sneaker clobbered Boomer's chin—he went over like an old dead tree.

Boomer lifted his hands in surrender. "Okay, okay—that's enough. I'm busted, man. I want to see my lawyer."

Nancy knelt beside him. "Boomer, I'm not a cop."

"We're just concerned citizens," Ned added, coming up behind them and pinning him to the floor.

53

"Then how about letting me go?" Boomer tried to sit up.

"After you put a gun to Nancy's head? No way, pal!"

"Boomer, we've got you cold on assault and unlawful possession of a gun." Reaching across the floor, Nancy retrieved her shoulder bag. "Tell you what, though. If you'll answer a few questions for me, I won't mention that you took aim at that black-haired guy."

"All right." Boomer sighed. "Ask your questions."

Nancy took the photo of Lisa Trumbull out of her bag. "Have you ever seen this girl before?"

"Yeah, I've seen her." He tilted the photo slightly. "She came up to me on Waikiki Beach yesterday. Two o'clock or so. She wanted to sell me a diamond. Real quality stuff, too. I offered to set up a meet, but she wouldn't go for it. She said she'd make the arrangements." He lowered his voice. "Look, don't go spreading this around, okay? I don't want people to think I'm a double-dealer." He sat cross-legged on the hallway floor. "The whole scene felt wrong, you know? She didn't seem like the type to be fencing diamonds. I thought maybe it was a cop setup. So I followed her."

"Where did she go?" asked Nancy eagerly.

"A rundown apartment house. The Ka Lae, it's called."

Suddenly a pair of uniformed security men

rushed up to them. "What's the problem here, miss?"

"This man pulled a gun on me in the garage," Nancy explained, brushing her hair back. "Place him under arrest."

The guards hauled Boomer to his feet. He struggled in their grip, yelling, "Hey! Where's my lawyer, man?"

"We'll need to ask you a few questions, miss," one guard called back over his shoulder. "Could you come with us?"

"Be glad to," Nancy answered. But as she and Ned followed, she was worrying about the moon-faced man. Who was he? First he'd been watching Lisa's apartment. Then he'd shown up at the garage. And judging from his reaction to Boomer's threat, Nancy had been his quarry.

A sudden chill touched Nancy's heart. There were too many wild cards in the Lisa Trumbull case. The Malihini Corporation was one. That moon-faced man was the other. Were the two connected? Or were they operating independently?

Either way, Nancy knew, she had to fit those puzzle pieces into their proper places. Otherwise, she and her friends might not get out of this alive!

"Uh-oh! Looks like there's roadwork up ahead," Nancy announced.

They were heading north to Honolulu's financial district. Long, low-roofed bungalows from the 1940s flanked the street on either side, a reminder of the days when Paawa had been a suburb of the city.

"How bad is it?" asked Bess.

Nancy stuck her head out the side window. Up ahead, the line of traffic was snaking around a city water department excavation. Propped up against a sawhorse was a huge sign: WARNING! EXPLOSIVES IN USE! TURN OFF YOUR RADIO!

"Slow going, but we'll get there." Nancy put the car in neutral.

"We should've called George at the bank. Let her know we're coming," Bess observed. "You know how she hates to be kept waiting."

Nancy sighed. "It can't be helped. I'm sure she'll understand."

"What's the next stop after the bank?" asked Ned.

"The Ka Lae apartment house." Nancy frowned in determination. "I want to see how reliable Boomer's information is."

The car ahead of them lurched forward. Nancy shifted into gear. then pressed the gas pedal. As their car rolled forward, she checked the dashboard, making certain that their radio was off.

The flagger waved his red banner back and forth. Beside him stood a mammoth pile of black volcanic sand. Halfway up the pile sat a small battery-powered lantern.

Suddenly the lantern's bulb turned bright red.

Nancy spotted it at the same moment the flagger did. Dropping his banner, he made shoving motions at Nancy's car. "Go back! Go back!"

Whonk-whonk-whonk! A klaxon bleated a deafening tone.

Uttering a cry of alarm, the flagger threw himself on the ground.

Bess blinked in bewilderment. "Nancy, what's going on?"

Nancy shoved the gearshift into reverse just as a fireball erupted from the pit, hurling a shower of debris straight at them!

Chapter

Eight

DUCK!" NANCY YELLED.

Covering her head, she leaned against the steering wheel. Ned braced himself behind the glove compartment. Bess plunged down behind the front seat.

The blast wave bounced the car on its springs. Rock fragments spattered the roof and hood, and the stench of burnt TNT permeated the air.

Coughing, Nancy switched off the engine. "Everybody all right?"

Ned got back into his seat. "I'm fine," he murmured.

"No injuries here," Bess said. "Nancy, what was *that?*"

The flagger came running, with a police officer right behind. The construction crew stood farther away, jabbering in confusion.

"Are you kids okay?" the cop asked. The name tag above his silver badge read "Pukui."

"Nobody hurt," Nancy reported. "Just a little shaken up."

Hands on his gun belt, Officer Pukui asked, "What happened here?"

"A TNT excavation charge went off," the flagger said, gesturing at the smoking trench. "Good thing the work crew was on break." He glanced at Nancy. "Didn't you see the sign? Why didn't you turn off your radio?"

"My radio wasn't on," Nancy replied.

"It must've been. The charge can't go off by itself!"

"Are you certain of that?" asked Officer Pukui.

"Positive!" The flagger lifted the brim of his safety helmet. "The charge was armed with a radio detonator. If someone comes too close with an FM radio, the signal can set it off."

Officer Pukui sat behind the steering wheel and turned the ignition key. The engine purred to life. "She's right. The radio wasn't on," he told the flagger. He turned to Nancy. "Did you leave anything in the trunk? A transistor radio from the beach, maybe?"

"This is a rental car. We haven't even opened the trunk!" Nancy replied.

The cop switched off the ignition. "I'm going

to try something." He lifted his walkie-talkie from his gun belt and turned it on. Static crackled harshly. His thumb turned the dial. All at once, a pulsing squeal burst out of the speaker. "Something in this car is broadcasting at seventeen hundred and sixty-eight megahertz. That's what set off the TNT," the officer said grimly.

"Ned, Bess—help me look," ordered Nancy.

"Got it!" Ned announced after a minute of searching the underside of the seats. He withdrew his hand to show them a small electronic device. The unit was the size of a cigarette case. A tiny operating light on its side glowed green.

"May I?" Nancy took the unit and examined it closely. Two inscriptions were stamped into the black vinyl—one in Japanese, the other in English. The English phrase read "Higashi Electronics, Ltd.—Osaka."

"What is it?" asked Bess.

"A radio transceiver—a bug," Officer Pukui said, taking it from Nancy. "Higashi specializes in this miniature stuff. This baby can probably transmit fifty miles."

Fifty miles, Nancy mused. That would cover all of Oahu!

"I sure hope this wasn't someone's idea of a joke," the cop said. "Letting you drive around with a live transceiver under your seat. That explosive charge could have killed you *and* a whole lot of innocent bystanders."

Satisfied that Nancy and her friends were not

at fault, Officer Pukui took their statements and gave them the transceiver. They continued on their way after Nancy had disabled the bug.

As they drove through downtown Honolulu, Ned said, "Nancy, do you think that was done on purpose? Did somebody try to get us blown up?"

Nancy shook her head. "I doubt it. For one thing, they had no way of knowing we would drive by *any* construction site, let alone that one. No, somebody decided to eavesdrop on us."

"When do you think it was planted?" asked Bess.

"Probably last night. Anybody could have walked by our car in the Ala Wai lot, opened the door, and stuck that thing under the seat."

Ned cast her a curious sidelong look. "Do you think it might have been someone from the Malihini Corporation?"

"Could be. Or it could just as easily have been the moon-faced man. Or somebody else." Nancy let out a deep sigh. "All we really know is, someone is awfully interested in what we talk about! Let's go pick up George."

Her face was grim. Someone was hunting them—that was certain. Some faceless, ruthless enemy was tracking them back and forth across the island.

And Nancy hadn't the slightest idea where that enemy would strike next.

* * *

The Windward Fidelity Bank was a sleek, clean-lined monolith that dominated the business district. After Nancy had parked the car, the three of them dashed across the boulevard and strolled into the airy lobby of the bank.

The tellers' windows were packed with customers, so Nancy tried the loan section. A good-looking young man with chestnut hair was leaning over a calculator at the main desk.

Nancy cleared her throat. "Excuse me."

He looked up and smiled. "Hi! What can I do for you?"

"I'm Nancy Drew." She gestured at her friends. "Bess Marvin—Ned Nickerson. We'd like to see Mr. Rafferty, please."

"Oh, of course! You're with George. She's upstairs with the Old Man right now." Rounding the desk, he extended a welcoming hand. "I'm Jack Showalter, junior accountant."

"Have you worked here long?" asked Nancy.

"Since June. I just graduated from business school." Jack picked up his telephone. "Let me call the Old Man for you."

Jack buzzed Mr. Rafferty's secretary and told her that Nancy had arrived. Then, looking puzzled, he hung up.

"What is it?" Nancy asked.

"Odd. She said he'd be down in person," Jack replied. "Mr. Rafferty *never* does that!"

Bess pointed at the elevator. The green light

descended the row of numbers. "Here he comes."

The elevator doors slid open. Nancy found herself staring at an irate middle-aged man in a navy blue pin-striped suit. Ross Rafferty was a slim, vain-looking man, with pudgy jowls and thick auburn hair combed into an unlikely pompadour.

Then Nancy noticed the men in the elevator with him. Big, competent-looking bank guards. They had their guns out.

"That's them!" Ross Rafferty pointed at Nancy. "Place those kids under arrest!"

Chapter

Nine

Under arrest?" echoed Bess.

The bank guards surrounded them.

"Bring the other one," Ross Rafferty ordered.

A tough-looking guard ushered George out of the elevator. Her eyes blazed furiously as she looked at the banker. "Mr. Rafferty, your hospitality leaves something to be desired."

Facing him, Nancy said, "Mr. Rafferty, my friends and I were hired to find your stepdaughter."

"I know who you are." Mr. Rafferty flexed his shoulders arrogantly. "You private eyes are all alike. This is nothing but a cheap shakedown."

Nancy blinked in disbelief.

64

"I know how you people operate," Rafferty continued. "You've conned poor Alice into thinking you can help. You'll feed her little bits of information—just enough to keep her anxious. Then you'll milk this—this situation—for years!"

Anger colored Nancy's face. "That is untrue —and unfair, Mr. Rafferty!"

"Save your breath!" Rafferty looked highly pleased with himself. "I've got you all now, and I'm going to turn you over to the police!"

Nancy managed to stay calm. "Mr. Rafferty, I intend to find Lisa—with or without your cooperation. Frankly, I'd rather work with you than have to tell Mrs. Faulkner you wouldn't cooperate." She pointed at Jack Showalter's phone. "So why don't you give her a call and tell her what you think?"

She could see that she had called his bluff. As the leading shareholder in Windward Bancorp, Alice had the power to fire him instantly. Which meant Rafferty didn't dare defy her!

"We'll see about that!" he said huffily.

Nancy watched as he picked up the telephone and dialed the Faulkner estate. "Hello, Alice? Ross Rafferty here. I've captured that girl who was conning you. With your permission, I'll turn this Nancy Drew over to the—"

Ross Rafferty wilted like a balloon with the air leaking out. "But—but—but—!" He sounded like an old motorboat.

"Yes, Alice. Of course, Alice. Good day!" Ross hung up quickly. He pressed a crumpled handkerchief to his lips, then turned to face Nancy and her friends. "Ahem! Perhaps I was a little brusque before."

He dismissed the bank guards, then told Jack Showalter, "I'd like you to serve as the bank's liaison in this matter." Turning to Nancy, he said, "Since we have to work together on this, I suppose we should make the best of it." He spread his hands in mock invitation. "How can I help?"

"I'd like to look at the safety deposit vault, if you don't mind." Nancy circled the table. "And I'd like to ask you a few questions."

Ross Rafferty led them all downstairs. The vault was as large as a barn, with a huge circular door. Inside, a tall Japanese man was examining some papers. He had iron-gray hair, a bristling mustache, and mournful eyes that reminded Nancy of a basset hound's.

"Nancy, this is Mitsuo Kaimonsaki, the president of the bank." Ross caught Nancy's questioning glance and explained, "I'm chief executive officer of the company that owns the bank. Mitsuo here is in charge of the day-to-day operations of the bank itself."

Mr. Kaimonsaki cocked a slim eyebrow. "This is related to the matter of Mrs. Faulkner's granddaughter?"

"Yes," Nancy replied. "Mr. Kaimonsaki, did

you suspect anything Friday when you let Lisa into this vault?"

"Not at all," he answered. "Lisa ran errands for her mother on several occasions."

That fit with what Diana had told Nancy. "Tell me, who had access to Ms. Faulkner's safety deposit box?"

Rafferty seemed to bristle at the phrase "Ms. Faulkner." Nancy guessed that the divorce hadn't been his idea.

"The immediate family," Kaimonsaki replied. "Alice, Diana, and Lisa. Bank employees need authorization to enter the vault—a pass signed by the three highest officers of the bank. The officers, of course, have routine access to the safety deposit boxes."

"Who are they?" asked Nancy.

"Myself, Mr. Rafferty, and Amy Sorenson, the bank's vice-president."

Nancy nodded in understanding. "Could I talk to Ms. Sorenson?"

"Perhaps later. She'll be back soon." Kaimonsaki looked apologetic.

Ross Rafferty fingered his tie. "Mitsuo, why don't you show Nancy's friends around the bank? She and I have to talk."

As soon as the others had gone, Rafferty said, "Nancy, I'm afraid I may have given you the wrong impression a little while ago." He smiled feebly. "We've all been under such a strain these past few days. Some of us more than others."

Nancy said nothing. Rafferty rushed to fill the conversational gap. "I—I don't know what Diana may have told you, but, well—I'm quite fond of Lisa, even if she isn't my natural daughter. I want Lisa home safe and sound. The same as you and Alice."

Nancy wasn't convinced. "Mr. Rafferty," she asked, "why didn't you want to cooperate with me?"

"I was afraid your involvement in this matter would upset an already delicate situation. The bank has certain—difficulties. I'm not at liberty to discuss them. Forgive me. Of course, I'm willing to give you all the help I can."

Sure you are! Nancy thought tartly. She was remembering what Dawn Burnham had told her about Lisa's home life. Ross Rafferty would never win a Father of the Year award!

Nancy wondered if Ross's "difficulties" had something to do with his stepdaughter's disappearance. Was Ross Rafferty a man with a closet full of nasty secrets?

Would one of those secrets get poor Lisa killed?

The Ka Lae was an old hotel, a 1920s tourist mecca that had fallen upon hard times. Still, its whitewashed facade, Moorish arches, and lush garden made it stand out in its rundown neighborhood.

George reached for her door handle. "Let's wrap this up."

"Not so fast, George," Nancy said softly. "I think maybe we'd better try a soft probe first. You know, the more I learn about this case, the less I'm certain of. Someone's trying to keep us away from Lisa. Why?" She glanced at each of her friends. "Both Alice and Ross mentioned business difficulties. How do they fit into Lisa's disappearance?"

"I thought Lisa ran away," George commented.

"So did I, at first. Now I'm not so sure." Nancy studied the front entrance. "Lisa couldn't afford airfare to get to San Francisco, right? Then how can she afford to stay *here?*"

"You're right, Nan," added Bess. "She didn't sell anything to Boomer."

"Bess, I need you and George for a diversion," Nancy said, opening her car door. "Get the desk clerk out of the lobby for a few minutes, okay?"

"You bet!" Bess said enthusiastically. "The Undercover Cousins strike again."

Nancy and Ned waited until the cousins had entered the lobby, then strolled up the front walk. Ned lingered at the right side of the entryway. Nancy peeked around the door jamb. She heard a TV set somewhere in the lobby.

"Kilauea volcano erupted today, spewing tons of lava into the air. Geologists say this is the biggest eruption in ten years. . . ."

Nancy tuned out the broadcast, straining to hear the girls' conversation with the desk clerk.

"What can I do for you, ladies?"

"My cousin and I are looking for an apartment," George said.

"Well, you girls are in luck. I've got three vacancies. Let me shut this thing off, and I'll show you around."

"Observers report volcanic blasts sixty feet high . . ."

Click! The TV died. "This way. Hey, what do you girls think of our volcano, eh?" asked the clerk.

Bess chuckled nervously. "I'm glad I don't live next door to it!"

Their footsteps receded into the distance. Nancy peered around the corner. The lobby was completely deserted. "They've gone. Let's go!"

Dashing quietly across the lobby, Nancy reached the desk and turned the guest register around. A name jumped out at her. *L. Faulkner!*

Nancy lifted the master key from its wall peg. "It's got to be Lisa," she whispered. "She's using her mother's maiden name."

Minutes later Nancy and Ned arrived at Room 232. Nancy eased the key into the lock and pushed the door open. "Lisa?"

Nancy switched on the overhead light, then gasped.

The apartment was completely deserted!

Nancy and Ned walked through the living

room, looking around in confusion. Not a stick of furniture in sight. The place had been picked clean!

Kneeling, Nancy ran her fingertips along the floor. "The floor's just been waxed. Somebody cleaned out this place very thoroughly. Let's have a look around."

They split up. Ned took the bedroom. Nancy checked the kitchen. Every wall and floor had been washed. They couldn't even find a stray fingerprint.

Frustrated, Nancy headed for the living room again. Lisa couldn't have cleaned this apartment all by herself. Indeed, why would she even bother?

Nancy suddenly remembered the transceiver in their car. She distinctly recalled having mentioned the Ka Lae by name. Now it was clear. Someone had tipped off Lisa and warned her to leave.

Another—more ominous—thought entered Nancy's mind. Suppose Lisa Trumbull had been *forced* to leave?

Nancy's gaze was drawn to the window. Gauzy drapes hung there, suspended by rings from an old-fashioned brass rod. The last two rings on the right were dangling—they'd slipped off the rod.

Rising on tiptoe, Nancy removed the entire rod. The brass was lightweight, probably hollow. An ornate bulb capped each end.

Somebody had taken this off the window,

Nancy realized. When they'd tried to put it back, there was nothing to use as a stepladder. They'd had to stretch, the way she did. Those last two rings had slipped off, and they hadn't bothered to replace them.

The bulb came off in Nancy's hand. Excitement set her nerves tingling. The curtain rod *was* hollow! And Nancy's probing fingers could feel something inside!

Tilting the curtain rod, Nancy withdrew a tube of heavy bond paper. As she did so, a smaller tube of onionskin paper slipped out and danced down to the floor. Puzzled, she picked it up. Then, tucking the onionskin under her arm, she hastily unfurled the bond document.

The corporate logo of Windward Fidelity Bank was the first thing that caught her eye. Just beneath, in bold type, was the message "You will pay to the bearer upon submission of this bond note the sum of fifty thousand dollars."

Chapter

Ten

NANCY'S BREATHING QUICKENED. This was one of the bonds Lisa ran off with!

"Ned!" she called in a stage whisper. "Come here—quick!"

Looking the bond over, Ned gasped, "Wow! But why didn't Lisa take this bond with her?"

"I'd say Lisa moved out of here in a hurry," Nancy replied. "She grabbed the curtain rod and shook out the papers. Only these two got stuck inside. . . ."

Ned pointed at the onionskin tube. "What's that?"

"Let's find out!" Nancy hurriedly unrolled it.

The paper was a shipping manifest. Nancy's

eyes skimmed the list of items. "Pieces of radio equipment," she said. Then the paper quivered in her grasp as she saw the name of the buyer.

Malihini Corporation
P.O. Box 4237661
Honolulu, HI

"Looks as if our two cases are coming together, Ned. There's our link between Lisa Trumbull and the Malihini Corporation."

"And our link with the transceiver we found in our car." Ned's thumb tapped the shipper's name. "Higashi Electronics."

Nancy checked the items. "You're right. There's the transceiver the Malihini Corporation ordered. So they're the ones who did it." She rolled up the two papers again. "First they tried to stop us from searching for Lisa. Then they tried to spy on us."

"I don't get it." Ned replaced the curtain rod. "How did a Malihini Corporation shipping manifest wind up inside a Windward bearer bond?"

"It has to be one of two things," Nancy replied. "Either Lisa found this manifest somewhere else and included it with her papers, or the manifest itself was tucked inside the bearer bond."

"For what reason?" asked Ned.

"Your guess is as good as mine. Let's go talk to the desk clerk."

Nancy and Ned left the building via the fire escape. They waited in the garden, watching Bess and George walk back to the car. Then they strode through the front entrance.

"Afternoon." The clerk smiled. "What can I do for you?"

As they crossed the lobby, Nancy took out her photo of Lisa. She put it on the counter. "We're private detectives. We're looking for this girl. Have you seen her?"

"Miss Faulkner? Sure!" He glanced at the photo, then handed it back to Nancy. "You just missed her. She checked out about an hour ago."

Nancy replaced the photo in her bag. "How'd she pay for the room?"

"Credit card. But it wasn't her credit card. It was charged to a company account—the Malihini Corporation."

Them again! "Any idea why Miss Faulkner left?" Nancy prodded.

"I guess it was because of that phone call," the clerk replied. "Came about four o'clock. I handle the switchboard and put it through. Next thing I know, the girl's bolting out of here. Didn't even sign out! Then the movers showed up . . ."

"Movers?" echoed Nancy and Ned in unison.

"Yeah, the same bunch that brought that furniture a few days ago. They had orders to clean out the place. Kahuku Moving Van Company."

"Thank you." Nancy stepped away from the

counter. "Listen, if you hear from Miss Faulkner again, please contact the Honolulu police."

"Why? What's the problem?" The clerk looked wary.

"She's a runaway," Ned answered.

"Okay, I'll call them."

His bland tone told Nancy that he wouldn't even try. A place like the Ka Lae wanted no trouble with the police.

Silently she followed Ned out to the car.

Outside, the Hawaiian night was cool and still. A golden glimmer rested on the mountains, the last remnant of sunset. Nancy quickly told Bess and George what had happened inside. Then, flushed with inspiration, she led her friends down the street to a corner convenience store.

"I've got an idea," Nancy murmured, checking the shopworn Yellow Pages at the pay phone. After popping her coins in, she punched in the numbers.

The phone at the other end rang twice. A woman answered. "Good evening. Kahuku Moving Van Company."

"Hi, I'm Lisa Faulkner," Nancy said, winking at her friends. "You people moved my furniture this afternoon. But you left my couch behind. Could you send your men over to pick it up, please?"

"I'm sorry, Ms. Faulkner, but you'll have to clear that with the people who rented the van."

Nancy experienced a tingle of foreboding.

"Uh, no problem." She waited several seconds, then added, "Oh, dear! I seem to have lost their number. Could you?"

"Sorry, Ms. Faulkner, but we have no phone number for them. Just their post office box." The woman sounded sympathetic. "Why don't you call the operator and tell her you need the number for the Malihini Corporation?"

"I'll do that. Thanks." Nancy hung up.

When Nancy had related the gist of the conversation, Ned said, "This is crazy! Why would a bunch of business people help a teenager run away from home?"

Bess looked around nervously. "I don't know about you guys, but I'm scared. Who are these Malihini guys? They set us up—planting stuff in our car! I don't like being a target!"

"Neither do I," Nancy said, rounding the front of her car. "I think it's high time we had a talk with Alice Faulkner."

"About what?" asked Ned.

"The business difficulties she and Ross mentioned," Nancy replied. "Every time we go after Lisa, we run smack into the Malihini Corporation. How come? There's a business angle to this case that just won't go away." She lifted the door latch. "And it's time we found out what it is."

The plantation house gleamed in the moonlight. Palm trees rustled in the soft breeze. As Nancy and her friends approached the house, a woman's silhouette appeared in the bright rectangle of the doorway.

Alice Faulkner leaned forward expectantly. "Nancy! Have you found her?"

Nancy felt miserable. Breaking this news was a hard thing to do. "I'm sorry, Mrs. Faulkner. Somebody tipped Lisa off that we were coming. It's just a temporary setback, though."

Alice's proud shoulders drooped, but she managed to conceal the extent of her disappointment. "Please come in. I do hope you'll stay for dinner. I could use some pleasant company for a change." With a weary smile, she led them to the dining room. "Ross and his associates are here. Trying to comfort me, or so they say. Personally, I'd rather have them out looking for Lisa."

Nancy stepped into the dining room, where vast sliding-glass doors offered a panoramic view of the palm-studded garden. Ross Rafferty stared into the night, shoulders tense. Mitsuo Kaimonsaki stood by the liquor cabinet. He was pouring brandy for a woman who was standing next to Rafferty.

The woman was nearly as tall as Mitsuo in her stiletto heels. An aquamarine cocktail dress molded her superb figure. Her beautiful face was framed by a tumble of stylishly coiffed blond hair.

Alice went right over to her. "Amy, I don't believe you've met Nancy Drew. This is Amy Sorenson, the bank's vice-president."

Flashing a warm smile, Amy nodded. "How do you do, Nancy."

"My friends—" Nancy gestured at her companions. "Ned Nickerson—Bess Marvin—George Fayne."

Amy's green eyes blinked in disbelief. Nancy sensed Amy's sudden coolness.

"You're George?" The woman's tone dripped disapproval.

"I have been all my life." George lifted her chin. "Do you have a problem with that?"

Looking a little embarrassed, Amy smoothed the skirt of her dress. "Er—no, it's just a bit unusual, that's all."

Holding a chair for Alice, Mitsuo remarked, "Why don't we start dinner? The food smells delicious."

Nancy and her friends enjoyed the old-fashioned Polynesian dinner: roast suckling pig with baked taro, cooked spinach, and *poe,* a starchy pudding made of papaya, mangoes, and bananas.

Midway through dessert, Nancy asked, "Mrs. Faulkner, what do you know about the Malihini Corporation?"

Clink! Ross dropped his fork, his eyes round with shock. Amy cleared her throat and lowered her eyes. Mitsuo stared quizzically at Nancy.

Alice looked troubled. "Nancy, where did you hear that name?"

Snorting in disgust, Ross threw his napkin on

the table. "Go ahead, Alice. Tell her! Then we can take out an ad in the *Star-Bulletin* and tell the whole world!"

"Mind your manners and hush!" Alice said sharply. "This is my home, and Nancy is my guest. I want to know where she heard about the Malihini Corporation." Alice looked at Nancy purposefully. "Well?"

So Nancy told her. When she had finished, Alice leaned back in her chair. "It fits. It fits so well." She closed her eyes in misery. "It's what I feared all along. They're using Lisa to strike at me."

"Who are 'they'?" Nancy asked.

"The Malihini Corporation first appeared in Honolulu a year ago," Alice explained. "They bought real estate all over the Islands. In time, they became Hawaii's biggest developer. But nobody seems to know who they are."

"Why are they after you, Mrs. Faulkner?"

Alice made a steeple of her fingers. "Our bank has been putting money into the Konalani project. It's a planned community on Oahu's north shore. We have a lot of money riding on the outcome of that project."

Ross thumped the table with his fist. "And they're trying to sandbag us! You see, Nancy, our bank has been having a serious problem with cash in recent years. The Konalani project will save us. But if our investors ever learn that the project is in danger of collapse, they'll sell their shares of Windward Bancorp stock!"

"You lost me," Bess murmured.

Amy smiled indulgently. "It's simple economics, dear. Windward Bancorp is the company that owns the bank. They have stockholders, just like any other company. If the stockholders dump their shares, someone else can buy them all up and take control of Windward Bancorp."

So that was why Ross Rafferty didn't want to go to the police, Nancy thought. The merest hint of Faulkner family trouble might trigger a panic among Windward stockholders. But how could he be so callous? There was no way the bank's well-being measured up against the life and safety of a human being!

Nancy's brow furrowed. "And you have no idea who's on the board of this corporation?"

"None whatsoever." Amy shook her head. "Believe me, we've tried to find out. No luck! Not even Lester could learn anything."

"Who's Lester?" asked Ned.

"Lester Jarman, my late husband's business partner," Alice explained. "He and Charlie founded Windward Fidelity Bank thirty years ago. Lester's retired now. He's still sharp as a tack, though. Next to me, he's the biggest stockholder in Windward Bancorp."

Nancy tapped her lower lip thoughtfully. So the Malihini Corporation was trying to steal the bank away from the Faulkner family. That made sense. But how was helping Lisa run away from home supposed to accomplish that?

Nancy shivered. To save Lisa Trumbull, Nancy would have to trail a pack of killers through the strange and treacherous world of high finance!

Chapter

Eleven

THE NEXT MORNING Nancy and Ned visited the main station of the Honolulu Police Department. A grizzled desk sergeant directed them down the hall to the office of the Criminal Investigation Division.

"Hi, Nancy!" Tim DiPrizio called out. He was in shirtsleeves, his feet propped on the desk. Martin Giles sat across the aisle, painstakingly typing with two fingers. "What brings you kids downtown?"

"We need some information, Tim." Nancy quickly explained how the Malihini Corporation had foiled them. When she had finished, Tim remarked, "Malihini Corporation, eh? Never heard of them."

"I'm not surprised," Nancy added. "They keep a really low profile. I was hoping you guys could dig up some tax information on them."

"Be happy to." Tim glanced at his partner. "You're the team intellectual, Marty. Where do you go for corporate tax records?"

"The state Department of Accounting and General Services," Martin answered, pulling on his suit jacket. "My friend Darlene works over there. Let me go talk to her. You folks sit tight. I'll be back."

Martin was as good as his word. He returned to the detectives' office an hour later and handed Nancy a slim manila folder. He wasn't smiling.

"That's a copy of the state tax file," Martin told her. "There isn't a whole lot on this Malihini Corporation. This just says they're an overseas investments firm. They don't even have an office here, just that post office box. According to Darlene, the Malihini Corporation was chartered in the Cayman Islands. They're very careful not to break any laws. They always pay their city, state, and county tax assessments. They always pay by mail, too, using checks drawn on the Bank of Nova Scotia."

Tim sat on the edge of his desk. "What's the bottom line, partner?"

Martin sighed. "These Malihini dudes are under a cloak of total secrecy. There's no way to get a handle on them. Compared to the Malihini Corporation, the mob is a bunch of blabbermouths."

Disappointed, Nancy handed back the file. "Thanks, guys."

Martin stroked his goatee thoughtfully. "Know what's bothering me?"

"What?" asked Tim, standing up.

The black officer's gaze shifted curiously to Nancy. "You tried to find these Malihini guys. No luck! I tried the state tax people. Nothing! So how did Lisa Trumbull find them?"

"Maybe they came to her," Ned offered.

"I think you're right, Ned." Nancy's voice turned somber. "No one tries to kill people in a rigged car accident unless they've got something to hide."

"You think the girl's in trouble?" asked Tim.

"I think she got in over her head," Nancy answered honestly.

As Nancy and Ned walked out the door, Martin said, "You kids be careful, all right? If you need any help, give us a call. I don't like the sound of all this."

Nancy slogged unhappily through the thick sand of Waikiki Beach. Two hours had passed since their visit to the police station. Since then, Nancy and her friends had split up, pursuing a number of different leads. Nancy and Bess were at the beach, interviewing lifeguards and surfers.

So far, it hadn't been a productive effort. Nancy had shown Lisa's photo up and down Waikiki, but no one remembered the girl. She looked too much like all the other teenagers wandering around.

Suddenly Nancy heard Bess's excited voice. "Nancy! Come quick! I found someone!"

Nancy trudged back up the sandy slope. Bess waited anxiously beside a tall surfer who was diligently waxing his board. "I figured you ought to talk to him, Nan. His name's Lance, and he's seen Lisa!"

Lance straightened up. With his well-muscled physique and skin the color of old hickory, he reminded Nancy of an ad for suntan lotion.

Lifting the photo, she asked, "Do you recognize this girl?"

"Yeah, I've seen her." Lance studied the photo carefully. "This morning. Just after sunrise. I was riding my board about a mile out. Pretty good surf here when it's high tide. Not as good as Kuilei or the Banzai Pipeline, but it's a wild ride coming in."

Nancy took back the photo. "Lisa was surfing?"

"Awww, no. She was with a big guy. They were walking on the beach. Like they were looking for something, you know? Then the big guy started yelling. The girl got scared and tried to run, but he grabbed her wrist. Then this car pulled up. A brown-haired woman got out and held the girl.

Meanwhile, that big guy went crazy! He was dumping out litter baskets—kicking the trash around. I figured the girl needed help, so I started in on my board."

"Then what?" asked Nancy, listening intently.

"The brown-haired woman got him calmed down. All three of them got in the car and took off." Lance's face showed regret. "They were gone by the time I got to shore."

After thanking Lance for his help, Nancy and Bess headed back to Kalakaua Avenue again. Nancy's thoughts were racing. What if the people with Lisa had been part of the Malihini Corporation? If so, they must have counted Lisa's money the previous night and come up fifty thousand short. They would have made Lisa retrace her steps, hoping to find the missing bearer bond —the one Nancy had found at the Ka Lae apartment house.

She explained all this to Bess, who asked, "Why would the big guy get so upset, Nan? It's Diana Faulkner's money."

"Bearer bonds can be cashed by anybody," Nancy replied. "The Malihini Corporation was planning to double-cross Lisa all along. I'll bet they promised Lisa they'd help her get to San Francisco to live with Michele." Nancy's stomach felt hollow. "Only I don't think Lisa realizes just how vicious the Malihini Corporation really is. She doesn't know how they've tried to hurt her grandmother. She probably thinks they're on her side, never realizing that they could turn on her at any time."

"At least Lisa's still alive," Bess added.

"As of this morning." Nancy flashed a worried look at her friend. "But you heard what Lance said. They're no longer treating Lisa like a guest. Sounds as if she's their prisoner now."

As they passed a dress shop, Nancy turned her gaze toward the window. She ignored the fashions on display, concentrating instead on the mirrored reflection of the street. It was an old detective trick, a way to check to see if she was being followed.

Ice water seemed to fill Nancy's veins. A familiar face had appeared in the crowd behind her. A moon-shaped face topped by slick black hair!

The International Market Place was just ahead. Nancy steered Bess toward the entrance. "We're being followed," she whispered, shepherding Bess into the mall. "I want you to go to a gift shop and pretend to be shopping. Make yourself noticeable. I want his eye on you."

"What will you be doing, Nancy?"

"I hope to set him up."

Nancy left Bess's side the minute she entered the gift shop. Nancy took cover behind a concrete pillar. Bess put on a nice show, playing the part of an airhead tourist. The man's face appeared in the window. Nancy flattened herself behind the pillar. His gaze on Bess, he moved farther along.

As soon as he was out of her line of sight, Nancy crossed the lobby and entered a phone booth. The phone at the other end rang sharply. George's voice answered. "Hello?"

"George, it's me." Nancy exhaled in relief. "Listen, our friend is back—the one with the moon face." Not pausing for an instant, she told George the plan. "I'm going to lead him back to the boat. You hide out on the pier while Bess and I go aboard. When the man leaves, I want you to follow him."

"All *right!* It's about time I got in on the action."

"Don't take chances, George. Okay?"

"Okay. Be careful, Nan!"

Nancy hung up. As she emerged from the phone booth, she saw Bess in the Market Place lobby wearing a floppy straw hat.

Her smile forced, Bess shifted her eyes to the left. "He's outside."

"I've set him up, Bess, but I'll need your help to pull it off. It's acting time again. Do a lot of talking while we walk. Tell me about Hawaii."

As they strolled back onto the sidewalk, Bess began a rambling monologue about beaches, gift stores, and palm trees. This left Nancy free to check the window reflections and make sure their enemy was still on the trail.

He was! The moon-faced man sauntered along, completely unaware that Nancy had identified him. Bess was doing a great job. Between her giggly chatter and Nancy's leisurely pace, the man probably thought they were out on a shopping trip.

When they reached Ala Wai, Nancy boarded the *Kahala* and pretended to check a mooring line. Bess went straight below. Peering out of the corner of her eye, Nancy saw the moon-faced man loitering at the dockmaster's shed.

Nancy went below. Hot, stifling air filled the cabin. She cranked open the hatch. A blast of cool sea air streamed past her face, filling the main salon.

Bess stood in her stateroom doorway. The giggling tourist was gone. "Nancy, is he still out there?"

Leaning against the bulkhead, Nancy eased the blind away from the porthole. Her gaze swept the parking lot. It was empty!

"Bess, I don't see him—!"

Thump! Nancy's gaze zipped upward. Something had hit the roof of the cruiser's main cabin.

The noise sounded like footsteps. And they were heading straight for the open hatch!

Chapter

Twelve

THUMP-BUMP-BUMP! NANCY LOOKED around desperately for a weapon. He was almost to the hatchway!

Something flashed through the opening. Gasping, Nancy raised her fist. The object struck the deck with a hollow thump, bounced toward her—and came to rest between her sneakers.

Nancy grinned. It was a white rubber ball covered with blue stars.

Bess groaned in relief and slumped against the wall.

A childish voice yowled. "Maaaaa! I *lost* it!"

"Jason, I told you not to play around other people's boats!"

Nancy returned to the porthole. She saw a tired-looking woman drag a sniffling toddler back to another cabin cruiser.

Across the lot, the door at the rear of the dockmaster's shed suddenly swung open. The moon-faced man appeared, wiping his hands on a paper towel. He crumpled it into a ball, lobbed it into the trash can, and moved toward the *Kahala.*

At that moment a brunette in a swimsuit approached from the other direction.

"George!" Bess gasped, standing at Nancy's elbow.

"I told her not to take chances," Nancy said in a worried voice.

As George approached the man, Nancy fretted. It was too late to warn her friend away now. . . .

"Excuse me. Are you looking for somebody?" George asked, her hands on her hips.

The man produced a battered wallet. "Yeah, you might say that." He flipped it open, revealing a laminated card. "I'm a private eye. I'm looking for Nancy Drew. You live around here?"

"Yes, I live here." Deadpan, George gestured at a big motor sailer at the end of the pier. "Lived here two years. Never heard of a Nancy Drew."

"Maybe you've seen her around, then." He put away his ID. "Tall girl. Reddish blond hair. Lives aboard that boat there."

"The *Kahala?*" George feigned a look of confusion. "That's Mrs. Faulkner's boat. Are you sure you're at the right marina?"

Nonplussed, the man pressed on. "Maybe you've seen Nancy's friends around. A blond girl. Couple of guys named Ned and George."

Nancy sucked in her breath sharply.

Mischief gleamed in George's eyes. "Hmmmm, maybe I have seen George around. What a hunk! He plays football for Oklahoma State." She grinned. "Want me to pass on any messages?"

"Ah, thanks—but no." Looking very worried, the man retreated across the parking lot. "I got to get back to work. See you!"

George watched him dash across the street and climb into the driver's seat of an older-model car. Tires squealed as he pulled away from the curb. George smiled and made a circle with her thumb and forefinger.

Nancy and Bess hurried out to greet her.

"If you want to find him, his license number is HWI zero-two-eight," George said, beaming.

"Nice work, George." Nancy hugged her friend. Then the three of them headed back to the boat.

Bess and George decided to return little Jason's rubber ball. While they were gone, Nancy, on impulse, flagged a cab and headed uptown. She had a few things she wanted to clear up before she looked for the moon-faced man. She had to learn more about the Malihini Corporation. Why did they operate out of a post office box? Why had they incorporated in the Cayman Islands? Once she was able to answer those questions, she hoped she'd be able to figure out what they wanted with Lisa Trumbull.

And Nancy had a good idea who to ask. . . .

Jack Showalter was on the phone when Nancy arrived. Flashing a welcoming smile, he gestured at the guest chair beside his desk.

"Yes, well, those interest payments are due, Mr. Gavalu." Jack made an apologetic motion with his free hand. "I understand. Yes. Nice talking to you, sir. Goodbye!" Hanging up, he let out a low groan. "What a day!"

"Who were you talking to?" Nancy asked curiously.

Jack flushed self-consciously. "The deputy finance minister of Kiribati. But he's not the high-priority item around here these days. Lisa Trumbull is. How are you making out?"

"Jack, have you ever heard of the Malihini Corporation?"

"Who hasn't? They're knocking the legs out from under this bank."

"Have you ever run into them?"

"Just once. I put together a nice little loan package a few months ago. I even got old man Rafferty to approve it. Then the Malihini Corporation came out of nowhere, stole my clients, and blew me out of the water!" Scowling at the memory, he added, "Why are you so interested in them?"

"I did some checking with the Honolulu police. They said the Malihini Corporation was set up in the Cayman Islands," Nancy said quietly. "You're the banker, Jack. Is there anything significant in that?"

Features thoughtful, Jack leaned back in his chair. "Caymans, eh? You know, those islands have the tightest bank secrecy in the world. Tighter than Switzerland! Some people use the Cayman Islands as a tax dodge. In my trade, we call it 'chasing the hot dollar.' What people do is go to the Caymans and set up their own private corporation. Then they open a bank account in the corporation's name, using a bank with a branch office here in the States."

"Like the Bank of Nova Scotia?" Nancy asked.

"Exactly!" Jack warmed to his topic. "It's a cute way to cheat the government. You make money in the corporation's name, squirrel it away in the Caymans, and, if you ever need any, draw it out through the branch bank. Let's suppose you made a million dollars, Nancy, and reported only ten grand to the IRS. How is the government going to prove you're a liar? It can't get into your Cayman bank to see how much you *really* made. That's what I mean—it's the perfect tax dodge."

Nancy mulled it over. "Jack, suppose you wanted to run your Cayman corporation out of a post office box. Could it be done?"

"Sure! All you have to do is set up either a telephone or a computer link with your Cayman bank. The bank will issue checks the minute you ask for them. Why, with computer equipment, you could run your corporation from the seawall at Sunset Beach!"

Nancy frowned thoughtfully. At first she'd assumed that the Malihini Corporation was based in the Cayman Islands. Now she wasn't so sure. The Malihini Corporation might be a front for someone in Honolulu. Someone very close to the Faulkners and to Windward Fidelity Bank.

Reaching across the desk, Nancy took Jack's telephone and tapped out the number of the Honolulu police's CID. Seconds later, Tim Di-Prizio's baritone voice answered. "Criminal Investigation Division."

"Tim, hi! It's Nancy Drew. Listen, I've got a lead. A license number. HWI-zero-two-eight. Can you run a make for me?"

"Just a sec." After a couple of moments, Nancy heard a police Teletype rattling noisily. When Tim returned, "We bombed out. That car's rented to a Waikiki agency."

"What about the person who rented it from the agency?" she asked.

Tim sounded frustrated. "The Department of Transportation lists only the owner—the Maka-

96

ha agency. To get the name of the driver, we'd have to subpoena the agency's records. We can't do that without a court order."

"Oh, well. Thanks, Tim. Bye!"

As she hung up, she noticed Jack's sympathetic expression. He said quietly, "You know, maybe I can help."

Jack picked up the phone and asked to be put through to Mr. Carstairs, the president of the Makaha agency. Then he switched on the speaker.

"Mr. Carstairs, this is Jack Showalter at the Windward Fidelity Bank. We have a little problem here, and I wonder if you could help us."

"Why, of course, Jack!"

"One of our stockholders had his credit card stolen," Jack said smoothly, giving Nancy a sly wink. "The thief apparently used it to rent a car at your agency. Our stockholder was billed for it."

Carstairs apologized profusely and asked Jack for the license number. Jack gave it to him. The phone was silent for several moments. Then Carstairs returned, sounding a bit confused. "Jack, that can't be right. We rented that car just yesterday to the Apex Detective Agency. The bill was sent to the Malihini Corporation. Are you certain about that number?"

Jack grunted. "Let me get back to you on that. Thanks a lot." Hanging up, he took a deep breath and expelled it in a long whoosh. "How was I?"

"Superb!" Nancy left her chair. "If you ever give up banking, Jack, you'd make a great detective. See you later."

"Take care!" he called after her.

Shortly before dusk, Nancy stepped down from the bus in Palama, a rundown neighborhood on the west side of Honolulu. She went to the address of the Apex Detective Agency that she had gotten from the Yellow Pages. The agency was located in a tumbledown office building on Vineyard Boulevard. She rode the dilapidated elevator to the third floor, her thoughts racing.

The Malihini Corporation must have hired the Apex people to search for Lisa, she mused. That's why I saw that moon-faced man staking out Lisa's apartment. Later, after Malihini had made contact with Lisa, they'd told Apex to follow me.

Well, two could play the surveillance game. Nancy intended to make certain that the detective agency was actually in that building. Then she would call in her friends.

The third-floor hallway smelled as if it had just been painted. Nancy sidestepped a full trash barrel as she left the elevator. Her footsteps sounded loud as they echoed in the empty hallway. The other side of paradise, she thought as she looked around the shabby surroundings.

At the end of the corridor Nancy found a frosted-glass door. The name read APEX DETEC-

TIVE AGENCY, with WALLY CERRADO—PRES. in smaller type.

Turning, Nancy returned to the elevator. Apex was here, all right. Now she and her friends would arrange a surprise for the moon-faced man.

She pressed the elevator button. Winches whined in the basement as the car climbed up.

Suddenly Nancy heard a footstep behind her. A broad hand shot out of the darkness, clasping itself around Nancy's mouth. The pungent odor of chloroform filled her nostrils. She kicked and struggled, but it was like grappling with a mountain.

Darkness rimmed Nancy's field of vision. Her knees began to buckle. Then everything went black.

Chapter
Thirteen

Nancy's mind groped its way out of the dark. She was vaguely conscious of motion and of sounds fading in and out. The distant cry of a frigate bird. The *thrumming* of tires on asphalt. The muted *ka-thump* of a car's automatic transmission shifting to a lower gear.

Slowly her eyes opened. She was lying on the back seat of a luxury car. The driver's head loomed above her, round and bald. She started to sit up, then felt a nylon cord wound tight around her wrists.

Looking out into the twilight, Nancy just caught a glimpse of a darker peak through the side window. We're heading into the mountains, she thought. I never should have gone to Apex by myself. Now the Malihini Corporation has me, too!

Minutes later the car slowed to a crawl, then stopped. Nancy heard the driver's door open and then close.

The rear door swung open. A shadowy hulk reached in. Nancy tensed, preparing to struggle, but the man lifted her as tenderly as he might a baby.

Outside, she got a good look at him. He was built like a pro wrestler, but his face had an innocent expression that didn't match his dangerous-looking bulk.

As the man strolled into the garden of a palatial estate, Nancy twisted and struggled. But she couldn't shake his iron grip at all. At last they came to a patio aglow with light from hidden lamps. Three people were sitting in white wrought-iron furniture, sipping tall drinks. Nancy recognized two of them.

Mitsuo Kaimonsaki and Amy Sorenson!

The third was a wizened, shrew-eyed old man whose Hawaiian shirt seemed one size too large for him.

Nancy's captor spoke. "I brung her like you wanted, boss."

"You did well, Oscar boy. Now, set her down," the old man said in a whispery voice. "Hello

101

there, Nancy. I'm Lester Jarman. I believe you already know my guests."

Jarman! Nancy remembered at once. C. K. Faulkner's old business partner, the retired co-founder of Windward Fidelity Bank.

"Oscar, untie Ms. Drew." Lester flashed a contrite smile. "I apologize for the melodramatic way you were brought here to Waikaloa, Nancy. But I think you can appreciate the need for secrecy."

Nancy rubbed her sore wrists. "Did anyone ever tell you that kidnapping is a crime, Mr. Jarman?"

"Seems I might have read that someplace." He sipped nonchalantly from his drink. "You know, you've got my people all stirred up, Nancy."

Folding her arms, Nancy replied, "Why don't you drop the act? It's obvious that you three set up the Malihini Corporation."

Lester Jarman winced. "I knew she'd say that." He turned to Amy. "Well, this was your idea. Would you care to set Ms. Drew straight?"

Nancy blinked in surprise. So these people weren't the Malihini Corporation! Then why had they kidnapped her and brought her here to Lester Jarman's estate?

"Allow me." Mitsuo put his empty glass on the table. "Nancy, some of us feel that you've been a little too . . . indiscreet in your investigation."

"Don't sugarcoat it like that, Mitsuo," Amy

interrupted. She glared at Nancy. "Look, you're upsetting far too many people these days!"

"You mean, like those in the Malihini Corporation?"

"That's exactly what I mean." Amy stood up suddenly. "I want Lisa back as much as anybody. However, I am *not* willing to see the bank destroyed in the process! Ross and Alice told you that our bank is highly vulnerable. The last thing we need right now is you blaring the name 'Malihini Corporation' all over the police teletypes!"

Nancy's eyebrows lifted at that. "And how do you know that I've been to the police, Ms. Sorenson?"

Amy Sorenson flushed slightly. "A pair of detectives came to see me this afternoon. Di-Prizio and Giles. They were not very polite."

Mitsuo Kaimonsaki said calmly, "I can assure you, we're not criminals. And never meant to hurt you." His hands fluttered slightly. "We only wanted to have a private chat with you. Please! Can't we keep the police out of this?"

Lester Jarman cleared his throat. His subordinates turned to face him, obedient and expectant.

"Mitsuo, why don't you go in and fix yourself another drink? You too, Amy. I'd like to talk to Ms. Drew alone."

Mr. Kaimonsaki rose immediately and headed

for the luxurious mansion, but Amy Sorenson loitered on the patio. "I wish you'd let me stay, Lester. I'm sure I could convince this girl—"

"Now, Amy, don't you fret. I can handle things."

Beep-beep-beep-beep! All eyes were drawn to the poolside table. The harsh sound was coming from Miss Sorenson's brushed leather handbag. Nancy glanced at the woman just in time to see an alarmed expression cross her lovely face.

No one moved. Lester said querulously, "Will you shut that beeper off?"

"Of course." Rushing to the table, Amy Sorenson grabbed the handbag. The sound died, and she set off for the house, swinging the bag casually.

"I hate those fool things," Lester muttered, shifting his position in the deck chair. He tilted his head toward the house. "Don't you mind them, Nancy. They're just worried about the Malihini Corporation."

"Mrs. Faulkner has better reason to worry," Nancy said, taking a seat. "They've got her granddaughter."

"So I hear."

"You don't sound too concerned about it, Mr. Jarman."

Reaching for his drink again, Jarman said, "Don't get me wrong. I like Alice. I do. I just never could understand her maudlin preoccupation with her family. Kids!" He snorted and took a sip. "Blamed nuisance. Worse than beepers. At least you can shut beepers off.

"Let's deal," Jarman murmured, a fiery gleam in his eyes. "You want something. I want something. You want Alice's granddaughter. I want the Malihini Corporation. I want them real bad, Nancy. *Nobody* tries to steal my bank away from me!" He licked his thin lips wolfishly. "You tell me what you've found out, and I'll tell you what you want to know. Deal?"

Nancy nodded. Then, keeping her voice low, she described her talk with Jack Showalter. When she was through, Lester Jarman chuckled and slapped his skinny thigh. "Cayman Islands, eh? Very clever! I thought Malihini was bribing our employees. But it sure looks as if there's a rotten apple in the corporate barrel, doesn't it?"

"Who could it be?" asked Nancy.

"Someone who knows the kind of bind we're in," he explained. "It all goes back a few years, Nancy. Ross Rafferty came over here from the mainland. Everybody said he was some kind of financial hotshot. He started lending money right and left to all those little countries in the Pacific. Then the world debt crisis caught up with them. The Pacific countries couldn't make their interest payments. We had no money coming in."

"That's what Ross meant by a cash problem," Nancy commented.

The old man nodded. "That's a fancy way of saying old Ross gambled on those Third World loans and came up empty. So Alice and me, we took control of the bank away from Ross and put all our remaining money into the Konalani project. When it's finished, it'll pay off big. We'll have enough to cover our bad loans and have a tidy profit, to boot."

"Then the Malihini Corporation mysteriously appeared," added Nancy. "And they began sniping at your project."

"That's right. What a coincidence, eh?" The old man tilted the brim of his Panama hat. "Ross is right, though. Whoever's behind Malihini wants our stockholders to dump their shares. Then they'll move in, buy them all up, and force me and Alice out."

"They?" echoed Nancy. "How many people could it be?"

"It's hard to tell. Ten—twenty—why, it could even be *one* person." He shrugged his thin shoulders. "Somebody who'd gone to the Caymans and chartered himself or herself as the Malihini Corporation."

Nancy stood slowly. "One thing still doesn't fit, Mr. Jarman. How did Lisa Trumbull get involved with the Malihini Corporation?"

"Good question, Nancy. Wish I knew. And now—"

Suddenly the bushes parted and Oscar appeared on the garden path.

Mr. Jarman finished his drink. "I expect you'll

want to be getting back to town, Nancy. Oscar will drive you." His lips crinkled in a wry smile. "I must say I've enjoyed our chat." As Nancy started down the path, Lester's voice brought her up short. "But watch yourself, Nancy. There are *sharks* in the water. It could be *anybody* behind the Malihini Corporation." His eerie laughter raised gooseflesh on Nancy's arms. "Why, it might even be me!"

Nancy said nothing during the long ride back to Honolulu. She was too busy thinking. Lester Jarman was right. Somebody at the bank was running the Malihini Corporation from behind the scenes. But who?

One by one, the suspects paraded through Nancy's mind.

Ross Rafferty? He was proud and ambitious. It must have really hurt his pride when Alice and Lester took control of the bank away from him. Not to mention Diana's divorce. Perhaps the Malihini Corporation was his bid to grab control of the bank and avenge himself on the Faulkner family all at the same time.

Then there was Mitsuo Kaimonsaki. What did he have to hide? She couldn't forget that it was Mitsuo who had originally let Lisa into the vault.

Amy Sorenson? As vice-president, Amy knew what kind of trouble the bank was in. She had the financial background necessary to set up a dummy corporation in the Cayman Islands. And then there were those instances of odd behavior from time to time. That episode with the beeper, for example. Nancy frowned suddenly, remembering her first meeting with the woman. Why had Amy reacted so strangely when she'd introduced her to George?

Lester Jarman? Nancy shuddered as she recalled his eerie laugh. The Malihini Corporation had plenty of money to spend. Lester was the wealthiest of the suspects. And the most ruthless, too!

Nancy's mind drifted back through the case.

Alice Faulkner? Probably not. Alice might have wanted custody of Lisa, but she would never endanger her granddaughter's life. She wouldn't leave Lisa in the hands of the criminals Lance had seen at the beach. Alice loved her granddaughter too much to ever consider that.

Diana Faulkner? This might be an elaborate scheme on Diana's part to keep custody of Lisa. Nancy hoped that wasn't the case. She didn't want to rescue Lisa Trumbull—only to send Lisa's mother to prison!

Oscar steered the limo into the Ala Wai lot. He got out and opened the door for Nancy. She didn't thank him. He muttered, "Evenin'!" and then got behind the wheel and drove away.

Nancy heard running footsteps behind her. "There you are!" Ned called.

She saw Ned rushing toward her, his arms

outstretched. Then she slipped into the comforting circle of his embrace.

"It's okay, Ned," she said in a small voice. "I'm all right."

Morning sunshine glimmered on the storefront windows of Vineyard Boulevard. Nancy leaned against a mailbox. In her pale yellow knit top and white jeans, she looked like a high school student.

Ned ambled across the street, grinned at her, and looked at his wristwatch. "Almost time. Any sign of Tim and Martin?"

"Not yet." Nancy glanced up the street. "Are Bess and George all set?"

"George is all ready, upstairs," Ned replied. "She signaled me from the hallway window. Our friend is in his office."

"And Bess is watching the alley, just in case he tries to leave that way." Shading her eyes, Nancy peered down the boulevard. "Oh, here they come."

A large sedan rolled up to the curb. Martin got out first. "Hi, Nancy. Is he upstairs?"

"Uh-huh. Are you all set?"

Tim got out of the car. "We'll go in first. Give us five minutes alone with him, then come on up. Having you walk in should really spook him."

Nancy nodded. "Okay, guys. Good luck."

Ned and Nancy waited breathlessly at the

front door. Long minutes passed. Ned kept glancing at his watch. Nancy breathed deeply.

Any minute now . . .

Suddenly Nancy heard a sharp, terrified scream. It was coming from the rear of the building—coming from Bess!

Chapter
Fourteen

THIS WAY! HURRY!" Nancy pointed to a narrow alleyway beside the building. She and Ned raced down it. Just ahead, they saw Bess grappling with the moon-faced man.

The man looked up and saw them coming. Shoving Bess aside, he ran to the high chain-link fence, jumped up, and frantically tried to pull himself up to it.

There was an aluminum trash can at the corner of the building. Grabbing the lid, Nancy cocked her arm and let fly. The lid sailed across the yard, hitting the man on the back of the head. Yowling, he tumbled to the ground.

Ned grabbed the man's shirtfront and hauled

111

him to his feet. Huffing and puffing, the man launched a shaky right at Ned's chin, but Ned ducked it easily and put him away with a solid right cross.

"Police! Hold it!" Tim's voice bellowed.

The detectives pounded down the fire escape. Tim held his .357 Magnum service revolver in one hand and his badge in the other. Martin vaulted the rail and dropped into the alley.

Grabbing the moon-faced man by the shoulders, Martin spun him around and pushed him up against the fence. "Spread 'em."

"Hey! What is this?" the man complained. "I haven't done anything wrong. Those kids assaulted me. Arrest *them!*"

"Yeah, you're a regular choirboy, aren't you?" Martin frisked him thoroughly. "Turn! Keep your hands up!"

The man obeyed meekly.

"Are you Wally Cerrado, president of the Apex Detective Agency?" Tim asked.

"That's me." Wally licked his lips in apprehension. "Look, I didn't mean these kids any harm. I was only doing my job."

"Why did you run away when you saw us coming?" Martin asked.

Wally grimaced in embarrassment. "Well, I owe a few bucks around town. I thought you guys were here to collect."

Nancy asked, "How did the Malihini Corporation hire you?"

"I—I don't have to answer that. You're not a cop."

"No, but if I were you, Wally, I'd talk to the young lady," Tim advised. "You picked the wrong client when you took on the Malihini Corporation."

"What do you mean?" Wally mumbled.

"Remember Lisa Trumbull? The girl they hired you to find? Well, they're holding her prisoner," Tim replied. "You fingered the girl for Malihini. So I guess that makes you an accessory, doesn't it?"

"I never came anywhere near Lisa Trumbull!" Wally's desperate gaze traveled from the cops to Nancy. "Come on, you guys. Give me a break!"

"Give *us* one," Nancy urged. "Tell us everything you know about the Malihini Corporation."

Wally thought it over for a long moment. Then he shook his head sadly. "I should've known it was too good to be legit. Okay, I'll play ball. Come on up to my office."

Minutes later they were all gathered around Wally's desk. He pulled his Malihini folder out of an old file cabinet and laid it on his well-used blotter. "This is everything I've got."

As Martin thumbed through the folder, Tim pulled out his notebook and began taking the private eye's statement.

"How did the Malihini Corporation hire you?" asked Nancy.

"They sent me a letter. Express courier, plus a retainer—a check for ten thousand dollars. They told me that Lisa had run away from home. They were sure she was still here in Honolulu, and they wanted me to find her. So I staked out the girl's condo. Asked a few questions around town. But she never turned up."

"Why did you start following me?" asked Nancy.

"They told me to."

"How?"

"I got another express letter from the Malihini Corporation. Haven't had time to cash the check."

"May I see them, please?" Nancy asked.

The check was for twenty thousand dollars, issued by the Bank of Nova Scotia in the Cayman Islands. Wally looked on in dismay as Tim put it into his plastic evidence bag.

Nancy's gaze skimmed the letter. It was on quality bond paper with the legend THE MALIHINI CORPORATION across the top.

Dear Mr. Cerrado,

We are highly satisfied with your work on the Lisa Trumbull case. Now, however, we have need of your services in a more pressing matter. We wish you to place four people under surveillance, two men and two women. They are: Nancy Drew, Ned Nickerson, Bess Marvin, and George Fayne.

We want no action taken against these people at the present time. We will be contacting you in the near future to arrange a time and place for the transfer of your information.

The Malihini Corporation

"I did like they wanted," Wally said as Nancy handed the cops the letter. "I managed to find you three." His face turned rueful. "But I never got a line on that George Fayne guy."

Running footsteps sounded in the corridor. A worried-looking George appeared in the doorway. "Nancy! I've been looking all over for you guys!"

Wally's mouth fell open. "Hey—it's the boat girl!"

"Wally—" Nancy tried not to giggle. "Say hello to George Fayne!"

A short while later Nancy drove her friends to the bank. As they cruised along, Ned said, "You're looking thoughtful, Nancy."

"Curious, isn't it?" Nancy glanced at him. "The Malihini Corporation hired Wally to search for Lisa. Then, after we arrived in Hawaii, they told him to forget Lisa and concentrate on us. Let's look at that sequence of events again, okay?" Nancy tapped her thumb on the steering wheel. "Diana sends Lisa to the bank. Lisa is unhappy and grabs this opportunity to run away.

She cleans out her mother's safety deposit box. Later that afternoon, Ross Rafferty checks the vault and discovers the theft. Ross tells Diana what happened. Diana calls her mother." She lifted a forefinger. "Now—very soon after all this, Wally Cerrado gets that letter from the Malihini Corporation. They tell him Lisa is a runaway and give him ten thousand dollars to find her. What do you get from all that?"

"Wait a minute!" Ned frowned thoughtfully. "How did the Malihini Corporation find out about Lisa so fast?

George slapped the front seat. "Of course! The Malihini Corporation is run by one of Windward's top people. I'll bet they were all in Ross's office when he phoned Diana."

"Second point." Nancy lifted her thumb. "How come the Malihini Corporation never bothered with Lisa before? One day, she's a nobody to them. The next, they're ready to spend ten grand to find her. Why?"

Ned laughed aloud. "I get it! Lisa cleaned out the safety deposit box."

"Right." Nancy nodded slowly. "It was only *after* Lisa cleaned out the box that the Malihini Corporation went after her. Therefore, Lisa must have taken something of theirs out of the box."

"But how did something of Malihini's get into Diana Faulkner's safety deposit box?" asked George.

"A member of the Malihini Corporation put it there," Nancy said grimly. "Remember that shipping manifest I found? It was concealed inside one of Diana's bonds. The culprit must have done that with all of Malihini's papers." She eased the car into a parking space. "The way I figure it, Lisa grabbed the Malihini documents by accident when she emptied her mother's box. She found them later. She's probably a bright girl and realized who was behind the Malihini Corporation. So she decided to contact that person and deal those documents."

"And that explains why Wally was hired so quickly," Ned added as Nancy switched off the engine. "The culprit checked Diana's box, realized the Malihini papers were gone, and set Wally on Lisa's trail."

"Right!" Nancy opened her door. "And once they had Lisa safely stashed away at the Ka Lae, they sent Wally after us."

As Nancy and her friends entered the lobby, they ran into Jack Showalter. His tense face relaxed when he spotted them. "There you are! Mr. Rafferty sent me down to intercept you." He led them to the elevator. "Mrs. Faulkner and her daughter are upstairs. It's—well, it's pretty bad, Nancy."

A ripple of dread ran through her. Are we too late? Nancy wondered. Is Lisa dead?

Arriving at the executive suite, Nancy saw

Alice and Diana by the conference table. Diana was weeping like a child.

Between her anguished sobs, Diana gasped. "This is all my fault! I failed her, Mother. Lisa wouldn't have run away if I'd made her happy."

"Don't blame yourself, Di. You did your best." Alice's eyes filled with tears.

Nancy hurried across the room. "Mrs. Faulkner, what has happened?"

Taking a golden bracelet from the table, Mrs. Faulkner gave it to Nancy. "This is Lisa's. I gave it to her last Christmas."

Suddenly Nancy noticed Ross Rafferty, Mitsuo Kaimonsaki, and Amy Sorenson. They stood off by themselves, looking glum and miserable.

Alice handed Nancy a letter. "Ross got this in the mail with it." Her voice broke. "They—they wanted to prove that they really have her."

Nancy's stomach turned to ice as she read the terse, cruel message.

Rafferty—
We've got Lisa. Here's her bracelet. If you call the police, she's dead. Here are our terms: You, Jarman, Kaimonsaki, Sorenson, and the Faulkners will sell your shares in Windward Bancorp to us at a price we will name. Or else you'll never see Lisa again!
                              The Malihini Corporation

Chapter

Fifteen

COMING UP BEHIND Nancy, Ross said, "We can't be certain that the Malihini Corporation has Lisa. This could be a bluff."

"Lisa loved that bracelet!" Alice snapped, whirling to face him. "She never would have given it up."

Ross didn't meet her eyes. "We can't sell those shares. We mustn't! It'll be the end of the bank!"

"The bank can go hang!" Alice declared, her eyes flashing. "If I have to sell to save my granddaughter, I'll do it!"

Ross looked as if he'd just been shot. "You —you can't do this to me!"

"You did it to yourself, you moron!" Mitsuo exploded, clenching his fists. "You and your grandiose schemes! Lending money to all those small countries. I warned you against it! You've ruined me, Rafferty!"

Ross's face turned lobster red. "I'll remember this disloyalty. I'll get you, Kaimonsaki!"

"Ross!" Amy shouted. "Don't you see? We *have* to sell! The girl's life is at stake!"

As the shouting continued, Nancy and Ned ushered the Faulkner woman out. Taking Diana's arm, Nancy steered her toward the water cooler.

Diana gratefully accepted a cup of water. Gone was the self-centered artist Nancy had met earlier. In her place stood a tense, frightened woman deeply worried about her daughter.

Diana looked at Nancy with haunted eyes. "My agent tells me that one of my paintings may bring two hundred thousand at auction." She sobbed. "Right now I feel like burning it! Why did I let my work come between me and Lisa? She's the most important thing in my life. Why did I have to lose her?"

Nancy squeezed the woman's hands comfortingly. "You haven't lost her yet, Diana. There may still be a way to save her. Will you answer one question?"

Sniffling, Diana nodded.

"What did you keep in your safety deposit box?"

Diana shrugged. "My passport, my jewelry, this and that. I'm afraid I didn't keep track. I left the money matters to my advisors."

"Who were they?" Nancy asked.

"Father left me a substantial portfolio. Mitsuo Kaimonsaki took care of it at first. He's been with the bank since I was a girl. When I married Ross, he took over my affairs." Diana blew her nose softly. "Since we were divorced, Amy Sorenson has been serving as my financial advisor."

Nancy gave her a quick hug. "Thanks, Diana!"

On her way downstairs Nancy mulled over what she had learned. Whoever was running the Malihini Corporation had used Diana's safety deposit box because that person knew she rarely went to it and knew *that* because that person had been her financial advisor.

Nancy stopped in Jack Showalter's office, but he wasn't there. Sitting at his desk, she opened her shoulder bag and spread the clues out in a semicircle—the Higashi transceiver, the bearer bond, the shipping manifest. Nancy looked over the manifest. "Telephone speakers, tape recorder, electronic beeper," she murmured to herself.

Electronic beeper! Amy Sorenson carried one in her purse!

Nancy frowned. She was just beginning to figure this out. Amy had thought George was a *guy.* . . .

Nancy picked up the bearer bond. Too bad Lisa didn't write a message on this, she thought.

She might have told us where she's being held —Nancy paused suddenly.

But the bad guys don't know she didn't leave a message, do they?

She grinned, folding the thick paper once more. An idea was beginning to take shape. It was risky—but if it worked, it would lead her straight to Lisa.

Picking up Jack's phone, Nancy said, "Operator, put me through to the Honolulu police, please."

An hour later Nancy stood on the foredeck of the *Kahala*. A familiar voice hollered a greeting. Turning, she saw Tim and Martin walking down the wharf. Tim carried a brown-paper package under his arm.

"Welcome aboard, guys. That was quick."

"We took off right after you called," Tim said, climbing on board. "This is a dangerous plan, Nancy. Be careful."

"I will." Nancy led them below. "Did you bring all that wiretap stuff?"

"That, and a court order." Tim patted his parcel. "Let's go to work."

They set up shop in the main stateroom. Tim unwrapped the package to reveal a tangle of wires, two plastic components, and a tape recorder. After checking the components, he hooked up the tape recorder to the boat's cordless telephone. Meanwhile, Martin looped the smaller wires over Nancy's head. She concealed them under her collar.

Ned picked up a small plastic component. "What is this thing?"

"A miniaturized tape recorder," Martin explained as Nancy clipped it inside the waistband of her slacks. "The other one's a transponder—it emits a constant radio signal. Helps us keep track of you at all times." He stood up. "There! You're wired, Nancy."

With the others at her heels, Nancy headed for the cordless phone. She tapped out the number of the Faulkner estate.

"Hello?" Alice sounded subdued.

"Mrs. Faulkner, it's Nancy Drew. Listen, you mustn't do what that note says. You mustn't sell those shares."

"But, Nancy, if it's the only way to save Lisa—"

"If you do it, they'll kill Lisa!" Nancy interrupted. "Once they have your shares, they won't need Lisa anymore. Don't you see?"

The older woman sobbed quietly. "What —what can I do, then?"

"Don't do anything for the next ten hours," Nancy pleaded. "Just please—please give me ten more hours to bring Lisa home."

"All right." Alice sighed deeply. "What you have in mind—will it save Lisa?"

"It's our only chance, Mrs. Faulkner. Now, one other favor. Take the phone off the hook.

Don't talk to anyone from the bank. No one! Not even the top brass." She licked her lips nervously. *"Especially* the top brass! Okay? I'll be back with Lisa in a few hours."

As soon as Mrs. Faulkner hung up, Nancy dialed the number of Lester Jarman's estate. Moments later, Lester's whispery voice came on the line.

"Nancy Drew! To what do I owe this pleasure?"

"Mr. Jarman, I am very close to nailing the Malihini Corporation. I thought you might be interested."

"I'm always interested in the Malihini Corporation." Nancy could see him at the other end of the line, leaning forward, eager to close another secret deal. "What have you got to trade, Nancy?"

"I picked up this little item a while ago." Nancy pulled the bearer bond out of her shoulder bag. "I called Mrs. Faulkner to ask her about it, but she's not home. It looks like a deed or something. There's a picture of your bank, and it says, 'Pay to the bearer fifty thousand dollars.'"

"A bearer bond!" Lester exclaimed. "It must be one of the bonds Lisa took from our vault. Where did you find it?"

"A surfer gave it to me." Nancy said, lying. She did not have to fake the excitement in her voice. "There's something on the back. Looks like handwriting."

"What does it say?" Lester gasped.

"That's just it. I can't read it. There's been some water damage."

"Water damage?"

"No matter," Nancy added. "We'll soon find out if it's Lisa's handwriting."

Confused, Lester replied, "How? You said you couldn't read it."

"I can't read it, Mr. Jarman, but the Honolulu police can. They can put it under ultraviolet light. Who knows? Maybe Lisa tried to tell us where she is." Nancy winked at her friends. "I'm going to the police station in a little while. Would you call Mrs. Faulkner and ask her to meet me there?"

"Nancy, this is splendid!" the old man cackled. "You did the right thing in calling me. Indeed you did." His voice turned thick. "I suppose you'll want some money for your trouble."

Nancy scowled. Perhaps Lester Jarman had never broken any laws, but he was a crook at heart!

"I'll get back to you," Nancy said sweetly, then hung up.

Martin was doubled over with laughter. "Nancy, that was one of the best con jobs I've heard. You had him all the way!"

But Bess looked bewildered. "Nancy, I don't understand. Why did you call Mr. Jarman?"

"I need Lester Jarman to spread a rumor for

me," Nancy explained. "Jarman won't keep it to himself. He'll call Alice first. But she's not home. He'll get frustrated. He *has* to check it out! So he'll call the bank. I'm betting he talks to one of them—Rafferty, Kaimonsaki, or Sorenson. They'll want to know why he's calling. Jarman will have to tell them about that bearer bond with the handwriting on it."

Ned's eyes flickered in understanding. "I get it now. The culprit knows Lisa was at the beach!"

"Exactly!" Nancy nodded. "And their imagination will do the rest. They can't be certain that Lisa didn't leave a bearer bond with a surfer."

"How does that help us?" asked Bess.

"Jarman will tell them I'm taking it to the police," Nancy replied, leaning against the helm. "Don't you get it? The Malihini Corporation has to stop me *before* I can get there. They have to come after me right now!"

George grimaced worriedly. "Nancy, you set yourself up as a target!"

Nancy shook her head. "They won't come here, George. They'll try to separate me from you. Then they'll make their move."

"All we can do now is sit and wait." Martin pulled a pack of worn cards out of his pocket. "Anyone for gin rummy?"

They started a game of cards around the galley table, but no one could concentrate. Finally Bess threw her hand in. "Nancy! This is killing me! What if you're wrong?"

"I'm not, Bess." Nancy rotated her shoulders, trying to ease the tension. "They have to grab that bearer bond before I get it to the police. The way I figure it, somebody will call and suggest that I bring it to the bank first. But it'll be a setup. Once I leave the boat, they'll grab me."

"But we'll be able to follow using the transponder," Tim added.

As Bess mulled it over, understanding blossomed on her face. Her gaze flitted to the cordless phone. She swallowed hard. "Then—then the person who calls is the *killer!*"

Nancy smiled wryly. "Not necessarily a killer, Bess. The culprit could always—"

Suddenly the phone cut loose with a loud ring. Nancy picked it up. "Hello?"

"Hello, Nancy." The voice was smooth and calm. "Amy Sorenson here. I thought we might have a little chat."

Chapter

Sixteen

WHAT CAN I do for you, Ms. Sorenson?" Nancy asked pleasantly.

"I've had some rather startling news. Are you alone?"

"Yes, I am."

"Good." Amy sounded relieved. "Lester Jarman told me about that bearer bond. I don't mean to tell you your business, Nancy, but I really think you should bring it here to the bank. It should be under lock and key."

"I agree, Ms. Sorenson. In fact, I was just about to call the police."

"Good idea. There's a safe in my office. Why don't you bring your evidence here and lock it up? Then no one can touch it until the police arrive."

Nancy feigned reluctance. "Well, I don't know . . ."

"Look, I'll send my limo right over. You call the police and ask them to meet you here."

"Sounds good to me, Ms. Sorenson. Where shall I meet you?"

"Oh, I won't be coming. Just look for my car—a beige limousine. My chauffeur, Ramon, will meet you right in front of the marina. Please be careful, Nancy."

"I will. Thanks." She hung up.

Martin ran a quick check on the minirecorder. It worked perfectly. Nancy clipped the transponder to a barrette and put it in her hair.

Ned and the cops followed her onto the deck. Tim said, "We'll be standing by, Nancy. If anyone makes a move to grab you, we'll bust them. Understand?"

Nancy nodded vigorously.

Ned's hand closed around her wrist. "Nancy . . ."

She turned to face him. "I have to do this, Ned."

"I know." Ned's lips brushed her forehead. "Lisa's out there, and she desperately needs help. Still—" All at once, he crushed Nancy to him. "I love you. Always have. Always will. Come back to me."

"I will. I promise."

Minutes later Nancy stood at the marina entrance, watching the traffic roll down the boulevard. Every sound seemed unnaturally loud. The rustle of palm fronds. The *chop-slosh* of waves against the beach.

Got to keep alert, Nancy thought. They'll try to grab me soon. This is the perfect time to do it—when I'm all alone.

Long, tense minutes passed. Then a beige Lincoln took the corner into the parking lot. Nancy caught a glimpse of the driver, a broad-shouldered man in a chauffeur's cap.

He rolled down the passenger window. "Ms. Drew, I'm Ramon Montanaro, Ms. Sorenson's driver. Hop in."

As Nancy opened the rear door, she noticed a pair of nylon-clad legs. Amy Sorenson's navy blue linen suit made her nearly invisible in the gloom of the back seat.

As she sat down, Nancy smoothed the back of her skirt. Her fingertips brushed the minirecorder, switching it on.

The driver did a three-point turn, pumped the gas pedal, and sent the limo speeding back onto the boulevard.

All smiles, Amy remarked, "Mind if I have a look at that bond? I can tell right off if it belonged to Diana."

After taking it out of her shoulder bag, Nancy handed it over. Eyes agleam, Amy studied the document, then flipped it over. Astonishment washed over her face. "What is this? There's no message on this thing!"

Beep-beep-beep-beep! Amy froze at the harsh sound. Nancy looked down at the woman's leather purse. "Aren't you going to answer it?"

Amy's mouth tightened. She said nothing.

"This reminds me of last night at Mr. Jarman's," Nancy observed. "You didn't want me to see your beeper then, either. Go ahead and answer it, Ms. Sorenson. I already know it's a Higashi."

Amy clutched the purse to her chest.

"The beeper's listed on the shipping manifest —the one you hid inside that bearer bond," Nancy added. "There's no need to pretend anymore. *You're* the Malihini Corporation."

With an ironic sigh, Amy reached into her purse, withdrew the beeper, and flicked it off. "I'll bet it's Ross. I knew he'd panic when he found his limo missing. I told him I was on my way to the Faulkner estate."

Nancy frowned. "It's all over, Ms. Sorenson. Tell me where Lisa is."

"Indulge *my* curiosity first." Amy tossed her hair insolently. "How did you know it was me?"

"The pieces were all there," Nancy explained. "It was just a matter of putting them all together. You're Diana's financial advisor. You knew she rarely went into the vault, so you kept all your Malihini stuff in her safety deposit box. Then Lisa cleaned it out. You panicked. Using your

131

Malihini Corporation front, you hired Wally Cerrado to find her." She took a quick breath. "After reading those documents, Lisa realized that you were the brains behind the Malihini Corporation. She came to you and offered to sell the documents."

Amy said nothing.

"You arranged for Lisa to stay at the Ka Lae. Then you heard that Mrs. Faulkner had hired me. So you set up that booby-trapped car scheme," Nancy continued. "When that failed, you sent Wally after me. But that's where you made your big mistake, Ms. Sorenson."

Confused, Amy stared at her.

"When I got to Honolulu, I had to sign for the car at Sunrise Rentals. I listed everyone in my party—myself, Ned Nickerson, Bess Marvin, and *George Fayne*. Sunrise sent a copy of that to the Malihini Corporation. When you read the names, you, quite naturally, thought George was a guy. Later, you passed on that bit of misinformation to Wally Cerrado when you sent him to spy on me. Wally was pretty surprised when I introduced him to George." She glanced sharply at the woman. "But not as surprised as *you* were! I wondered why you reacted that way at Mrs. Faulkner's. You were really shocked to find out that George Fayne is a girl," Nancy added. "After that, it was a process of elimination. The Malihini Corporation had to be either you, Ross, or Mitsuo. I knew it couldn't have been Ross or

Mitsuo. They had met George the day we visited the bank. That left you."

"Very astute, Nancy." Amy's face seemed hewn from ice. "Now what?"

Nancy looked her in the eye. "Just tell me where Lisa is."

"Not a chance!"

"Have it your way, then." Nancy tapped the chauffeur's shoulder. "Forget the bank, Ramon. Take us back to the marina. There're a couple of detectives there who'd like to talk to Ms. Sorenson.

Thump! The rear doors locked automatically. Nancy grabbed the door lever. It wouldn't budge!

"His name is Lew, and he works for me," Amy said, flashing a wicked smile. She took a small automatic pistol from the driver and leveled it at Nancy. "So you want to find Lisa, eh? I think we can arrange that."

The driver gave a sinister chuckle. He steered the limo down the off-ramp, heading for the airport.

Ten minutes later the car pulled up at a ramshackle hangar. Unfazed by the takeoff roar of the jetliners, Amy and Lew marched Nancy into the building. Turning on the light, Amy called, "Company for you, Lisa!"

Footsteps sounded behind Nancy. Turning, she saw a brown-haired woman in boat clothes and a teenage girl with brownish blond hair and striking blue eyes. Lisa Trumbull looked quite a bit different from her photos—rumpled, tired, and very, very frightened.

Amy smiled wickedly. "Has she been behaving herself, Marilee?"

"She knows better than to give *me* any problems," answered the other woman.

Lew locked the outside door. Nancy's gaze circled the room at lightning speed. Secondhand furniture. Heavy-duty wire barred both windows. *No way out!*

"Why don't you girls get acquainted?" Amy suggested mockingly. "I'll be back." Her two henchmen followed at her heels.

Lisa Trumbull eyed Nancy timidly. "Who are you?"

"Nancy Drew. I'm a friend. Are you all right, Lisa?"

"How—how do you know my name?"

"I'm a detective. Your grandmother hired me to find you."

Lisa's chin lifted warily. "How do I know you're not working for *her?*"

"You don't. You'll just have to take my word for it." Nancy drew the wire over her head, then wrapped it around the plastic case. She grinned at Lisa. "This is a miniature tape recorder, property of the Honolulu police. Now I've got to trust you. If you still think I'm Amy's spy, tell her about it. She doesn't know I was wearing it. Do you want to take that chance?"

Shaking her head, Lisa whispered, "No! I trust you."

"Good!" Nancy looked around desperately. "Where can I hide this thing?"

Lisa lifted the cushion of the beat-up sofa. "Here! Nobody will—"

Nancy heard the sound of high heels approaching. Hurriedly she tucked the minirecorder under the cushion, then smoothed it with her palms.

Amy strolled into the room. Aiming her pistol at them, she snapped, "On your feet, you two!" She glanced at Marilee. "Search and handcuff them."

The woman pinioned Lisa's arms behind her back, then snapped on a pair of shiny handcuffs. Marilee's hands drifted down Nancy's back. "She's clean!" Nancy shivered. Close call! If she'd still been wearing the minirecorder . . .

Amy gave the pistol to her henchman. "You know what to do with them, Lew."

Lisa spat, "You won't get away with this, Amy Sorenson!"

"I've already gotten away with it!" Amy flashed a tigerish smile. "You two are just loose ends that need tying up, that's all."

Marilee unlocked and opened the door. Lew shoved Nancy rudely. "Step lively there, Drew!" he muttered. "You're going sight-seeing— courtesy of the Malihini Corporation."

135

At that moment, an ominous noise overshadowed the background hubbub of the airport —the sound of a helicopter's rotor blades. A Huey helicopter touched down, and the side hatch slid open.

As Nancy climbed aboard, Lisa cried out, "Watch out for the doughnut ring!"

Quickly Nancy stepped over the thick circular cable on the floor. Then Lisa climbed aboard, followed by Marilee. The pilot turned in his seat, saw the girls, and frowned in bewilderment. "Hey! What is this? The boss told me cargo, not passengers!"

Lew put his pistol to the pilot's head. "Want to be a dead hero?"

Gasping, shuddering, the pilot shook his head.

"Smart guy." Keeping the gun on him, Lew climbed into the cockpit and buckled himself into the copilot's seat. "Get us airborne—fast!"

"I have to tell the tower our destination." The pilot flicked overhead switches. Turbines whined. The cabin began to shake.

"The Big Island." Lew pulled his seat belt tight. "I'll give you more details when we get there."

With a roar of power the Huey lifted off, rising slowly into the night sky. Nancy's ears popped. Peering out the side window, she watched the lights of Honolulu fall away. She knew the police hadn't had time to get to them. Amy had had them whisked away so quickly.

Sobbing, Lisa shook her head. "I—I've made such a mess of things. . . ."

Nancy tried to cheer her up. "You kept me from getting hurt a moment ago. How'd you know that ring was there?"

"This is an old army chopper. They used them in Vietnam. Soldiers used to clip their rappel ropes onto that ring and then slide down to the ground." Tears trickled down Lisa's face. "Nancy, I—I'm sorry . . ."

"Don't be." Nancy gave her a sympathetic look. "You didn't invent the Malihini Corporation. Amy did! She used you, Lisa."

"I realize that now." Lisa's voice was taut with anger and remorse. "I—I never meant any harm. Honest!"

"You can't give up hope, Lisa," Nancy said softly. "We'll get out of this, you'll see. I'm not the only one looking for you. My friends, your grandmother, your mother—"

"My *mother?*" Lisa echoed.

"You bet. Your mother loves you very much. You know what she told me? She said she'd burn one of her paintings if that's what it took to bring you home."

"My mother said that?" Lisa replied incredulously.

Nancy encouraged the girl to talk about herself. She knew that would keep Lisa from getting panicky. While she listened, Nancy's agile fingers explored the wall behind her, seeking an object

137

she could use as a makeshift lock pick. In a few minutes her thumb discovered a loose electrical brace—a tiny metallic pin used to hold the wiring in place.

Wiggling the pin into the handcuffs' keyhole, Nancy began working at it painstakingly. Easy does it! She closed her eyes. Any lock can be beaten, she told herself. All it takes is patience.

Over an hour passed. Marilee was no longer watching them. She slumped in her seat, sighing and dozing. Nancy managed to wheedle her pin past a tumbler in the handcuff lock.

All at once, a new sound intruded on the helicopter's droning—a low-throated rumble, like the thunder of a distant storm. The noise grew steadily louder. Curious, Nancy glanced out the side window.

Moonlit hills rolled away beneath the chopper's skids. Ahead, flashes of scarlet lit up the horizon. Then the rumble transformed itself into the earsplitting sound of gas explosions.

Nancy stared down in horrified fascination. Fiery sparks circled a cone-shaped peak. Plumes of red-hot lava shot into the night sky, and billowing clouds of steam drifted toward them.

"Kilauea . . . the volcano!" Lisa cried.

Lew left the copilot's seat. "Bring her right over it," he ordered. "Then hold her steady."

With a flick of his wrist, he disengaged the safety lock and pulled the hatch open. Stinking vapor flooded the cabin. "Come over here,

Drew." He flashed Nancy a grin of sheer evil. "I want you to get a real good look at Kilauea!"

Nancy fought down a surge of terror as she felt the lock's second tumbler give way. Her heart began to pound. One more tumbler to go!

Suddenly the helicopter swayed from side to side. Yelling, Lew grabbed a static line with his free hand. Its snap-link went flopping out the hatch. Aiming his pistol at the pilot, he snapped, "I told you to keep it *steady!*"

"I can't!" The pilot held the control column with both hands. "Too much steam! The up-drafts are too strong!"

Lew turned his gun toward Nancy. "Let's get it over with."

Nancy took a careful step forward. The pin began to slide in her sweaty grip. She felt faint. If she lost it now . . . !

Taking a deep breath, Nancy gave it one last solid push.

Click! She felt the handcuffs loosen on her wrists. Her right hand wriggled free.

Lew made a grab for her. "Come on, Drew! Don't take all night!"

Nancy let his hand close around her collar. Then, cocking her fist, she stumbled against him and planted a hammer-blow on his thigh.

Roaring, Lew collapsed on top of her.

Nancy chopped his Adam's apple. Lew gasped, tackled Nancy, and threw her to the floor. Nancy's knee bashed his stomach. Lew rolled away, his breath exploding out of him. His pistol swung toward Nancy. She threw herself on his arm, grabbed his wrist, slammed it repeatedly against the bench. His trigger finger tightened—

Blam! A bullet smashed the window beside Lisa.

Blam! A crater appeared on the back of the pilot's seat. His hands flew upward. "Aaaaaaaaagh!" he screamed.

In desperation, Nancy lashed out with a straight-legged kick. Her heel clobbered Lew's jaw, and he bellowed with rage. He rolled toward her, bringing his fist around in a vicious left hook. The punch caught Nancy on the chin. Next thing she knew, she was spread-eagled on the floor.

The pilot stood shakily, arching his back in agony. A bright red stain blossomed on his coveralls.

Still stunned, Nancy watched helplessly as Lew staggered to his feet. With a snarl of rage, he lifted his pistol high. He was about to crush Nancy's skull with a single blow!

That same second the wounded pilot slumped over the controls. The Huey's nose dipped suddenly. The floor tilted crazily to the right.

The momentum of Lew's upward swing threw him off-balance. He backpedaled awkwardly, like a cartoon character, heading for the open hatch.

Nancy saw him framed in the hatchway for a

split second. Then he was gone. His shrill death scream faded into the rumble of the volcano.

The chopper floor continued to tilt. Nancy realized that she, too, was sliding down the incline. The open hatch rushed to greet her.

The doughnut ring! she thought frantically.

Nancy lunged at the steel cable. She missed it.

With a wild yell, Nancy felt herself hurtling into space. The cabin's rim rode up her legs, over her stomach—all the way to her armpits. Lisa's terrified scream echoed in her ears.

Then Nancy was falling through thin air —right toward the volcano!

Chapter

Seventeen

Nancy had a sudden horrifying glimpse of Kilauea's fiery vent. Geysers of lava blossomed out of the crater.

All at once, the helicopter's skid swung into view. Nancy's clawing hand grabbed it. She dangled there for an impossibly long moment —buffeted by blasts of steam, watching the dark sky and the erupting volcano change places with each other. Then she doubled her grip.

Without a pilot, the Huey began to fly round and round in crazy circles. Nancy felt as if she were on a nightmarish merry-go-round. No way out this time! she thought, gritting her teeth against the blasts of steam. If the volcano doesn't kill me, the helicopter crash will!

She thought of Lisa, handcuffed and helpless—

Lisa! Lisa was a pilot! She could fly the helicopter and save them!

All Nancy had to do was get back inside.

But each turn of the chopper sent her swinging off to the side like a circus trapeze artist. Get back in? It was all she could do to hold on!

Just then something tapped her wrist. Looking up, Nancy saw a line dancing back and forth.

Nancy rode out the next freewheeling swing. Then, as her body slowed, she hooked her leg over the skid. Acrid smoke smothered the helicopter, and she felt faint. Her drenched hands began to slip. Uttering a breathless gasp, she shimmied down the skid and caught the line as it whipped past.

Nancy tugged on the line to make sure it was secure just as a glowing piece of jellied lava, as big as a basketball, splattered the chopper's belly. Nancy grabbed the line with both hands, her body spinning round and round like a yo-yo at the end of its string.

Wheezing and coughing, Nancy pulled herself toward the hatchway. Her grasping hands inched their way up the thick rope.

Now she'd climbed up past the skid. Her foot lashed out and caught it. That provided some support. Her head peeped over the rim of the hatch. Where was that doughnut ring? As she lunged into the cabin, her right hand closed around it. Thank you, U.S. Army! she thought.

"Nancy!" Lisa shrieked, bracing herself against the cabin wall. "The pilot's unconscious! Get me loose! I can fly this thing!"

The bucking helicopter was about to shake Nancy loose again. Summoning her last reserves of strength, she tightened her grip on the ring and pulled herself all the way into the chopper.

A jet of boiling lava sailed past the open hatch. Rising to her knees, Nancy slammed it shut. Then she crawled over to Marilee's jump seat.

Marilee was screaming hysterically. Nancy shook the woman's shoulders. "The key! Give me the key!"

"My necklace . . ." Marilee wailed.

The key dangled at the end of a tiny chain. Ripping it loose, Nancy stumbled across the seesawing cabin toward Lisa.

Lisa's handcuffs clanged as they struck the floor. On hands and knees, she and Nancy scrambled into the cockpit.

Lisa dropped into the copilot's seat. Her right hand seized the control column. Her gaze took in every flight instrument at a glance. All at once, the Huey stopped its mad whirling. Nancy helped the wounded pilot out of his chair.

"Nancy!" Wide-eyed, Lisa pointed at two U-shaped handles rising from the console beside her seat. These were the thrust levers, which controlled the power output of the chopper's twin engines. "Push those—*quick!* We're losing airspeed! If we stall, we'll drop right into the volcano!"

Now Kilauea's throaty roar smothered all sound. A titanic fire fountain gushed out of the crater. Hot lava spattered the Huey. The Plexiglas windscreen began to bubble and melt.

Grabbing the thrust levers, Nancy threw her weight against them. The helicopter turbines answered the volcano with a roar of their own. Lisa turned the control column to the left. The Huey veered away from the volcano, cutting a path through the swirl of steam and smoke. Nancy held her breath, listening to Kilauea's angry bellow.

Suddenly the steam outside the cockpit gave way to a star-studded sky.

With a sigh of thanksgiving, Nancy slumped to the cockpit floor.

When—if—we get back home, she told herself, I'm going to learn to fly a chopper. An airplane pilot's license isn't enough anymore.

Then she remembered the wounded pilot. Grabbing the microphone, Nancy chanted, "Mayday! Mayday! We have an in-flight emergency. Wounded man aboard."

"Tell them I'm heading for Hilo airport," added Lisa.

Nancy did so, then requested paramedics and

an ambulance. She tossed the microphone aside and grabbed the cockpit's first-aid kit. Pressing a gauze bandage to the pilot's bullet wound, she cast a final glance at Kilauea, now a fiery smudge on the horizon. The volcano thundered in farewell.

The next morning Nancy and Ned waited in the copying room at Windward Fidelity Bank. Peering through the little window, Nancy surveyed the vacant conference room. She smiled to herself, remembering the tearful reunion at the Hilo police station the previous night—how Lisa had rushed, sobbing, into the arms of her mother and grandmother. The expressions on the faces of the Faulkner women had made it all worthwhile.

"Think Jack will be able to lure them all in here?" Ned whispered.

"Sure," Nancy replied. "No one knows the Faulkners are still on the Big Island. They haven't heard from Alice since yesterday. They'll be here."

Muffled voices sounded in the distance, and the suite door opened. Ross, Mitsuo, and Amy walked in, trailed by Jack Showalter.

"What's this all about, Showalter?" Ross asked irritably. "And where is Alice? Not even Lester can find her."

"What did Mrs. Faulkner tell you, Jack?" asked Mitsuo.

Jack's face looked glum. "She's made up her mind. She's not selling those shares."

"That woman is a fool!" Amy cried. "She's doomed her own granddaughter!"

Then Nancy burst into the conference room. "Wrong! Her granddaughter's just fine, Ms. Sorenson. She's down in Hilo, safe and sound. Not inside the Kilauea volcano as *you* intended!"

Amy's eyes widened in disbelief. She whitened and swayed on her high heels. At that moment, Tim and Martin came through the other door. Tim set a tape recorder on the table. Martin flashed his badge, adding, "Honolulu P.D. Have a seat, gentlemen. We'd like you to hear something."

"What's the meaning of this?" Ross asked huffily.

"Ms. Sorenson is an embezzler," Nancy said. "She chartered herself as the Malihini Corporation, tapped into your bank's money, and used it against you."

Amy tossed her hair defiantly. "Preposterous!"

Tim took an onionskin paper out of his breast pocket and showed it to Mitsuo. "This is a shipping manifest made out to the Malihini Corporation. Look at the signature on the bottom. Whose handwriting is that?"

Mouth agape, Mitsuo stared at it. "It—it's Amy's!"

Martin asked, "Sir, will you swear to that in a court of law?"

"Let me see." Ross snatched the paper away. His face turned white. "Amy! What is this?"

"It's nothing." Amy sneered, glaring at Nancy. "There are no laws against incorporating yourself in the Cayman Islands."

Ross stared at her, aghast. "You betrayed us! You stole our money and used it to mess up the Konalani project. *You* tried to make the bank fail!"

"Prove it!" Amy spat. "There's no charge against me. I'm leaving!"

"Not so fast." Nancy slapped an envelope into her hand. "This is a warrant for your arrest."

Outraged, Amy flipped it open. "On what charge?"

"Attempted murder, kidnapping, and extortion," Nancy replied, folding her arms. "You're not going anywhere."

Her green eyes glittering, Amy ripped the document into little pieces. "It's your word against mine, Drew. No court will ever convict me."

"We'll see about that." Nancy reached across the table and flicked on the tape recorder. Amy flinched as her own voice filled the conference room.

"Mind if I have a look at that bond? I can tell right off if it belonged to Diana."

Amy stood transfixed, a look of mingled alarm and horror crossing her face. Nancy let it play until Lisa's voice came on, then switched it off.

"It's true you can't convict with just a tape," Nancy told the woman, "but when the tape is admitted with eyewitness testimony from Lisa and Marilee—well . . ."

Tim began the litany of arrest. "You have the right to remain silent . . ."

Nancy stepped aside to let them pass. A sullen, handcuffed Amy marched between the two detectives. The astounded bankers followed them out. Then, with a sigh of relief, Nancy squeezed Ned's hand and started downstairs.

The evening tide rolled into Ala Wai. Lounging in her deck chair, Nancy could feel the *Kahala* straining against her moorings. She grinned at Ned, who was setting their supper tray on the transom.

"Did Bess and George say what time they'd be back?" Nancy asked.

Ned handed her a hamburger. "Not really. You know how Bess is when she goes shopping." His eyes gleamed. "I won't complain if they're late."

Just then Alice Faulkner's voice called out. "Ahoy the *Kahala!*"

Peering over the rail, Nancy saw her on the walkway. Ned quickly put the supper tray aside, and he and Nancy hustled down to meet her.

"I came to say goodbye," Alice told them smilingly. "Diana, Lisa, and I are going on a round-the-world cruise." Her smile deepened. "Sort of a get-to-know-you cruise, I guess. We're going to try to be a family again. A *real* family."

"How are things at the bank?" Nancy asked.

Alice sighed softly. "Better. We took a little beating in the stock market when the news broke. But it wasn't as bad as it could have been." Then she took Nancy's hands. "I can't thank you enough, my dear. Because of you, I have my granddaughter—and my daughter—back again." Her gaze went from Nancy to Ned. "What are your plans now?"

"We'll be flying out in a few days," Ned replied. "Heading back to River Heights."

There was a merry twinkle in Alice's eyes. "Well, since you'll be here in the Islands for a bit, why don't you take the *Kahala* out on the open sea?"

Nancy blinked in surprise. "Mrs. Faulkner, that's awfully generous of you, but we couldn't—"

"I insist." Alice pressed an ignition key into Nancy's hand. "Go on. You earned it. Consider it a bonus for a job well done. You might consider sailing to Maui," Alice added, a fond smile on her lips. "My late husband and I loved that trip."

Then she walked back to the parking lot, her step as light and lively as a young girl's.

Nancy and Ned stood alone on the wharf. A

breeze stirred Ned's hair. He smiled, sliding his hands around Nancy's waist.

"I wonder what Maui looks like in the moonlight," he whispered.

Nancy lifted her face, waiting to receive his kiss.

"Let's find out, Ned."

Nancy's next case:

When Ned asks Nancy out for a really special evening, she doesn't anticipate anything out of the ordinary. But the date *is* special—Ned asks Nancy to marry him. Nancy considers his offer, but although she's sure she loves him, she feels the timing isn't right. Ned seems broken up, but at a party the next night he announces his engagement to Jessica Thorne, a girl Nancy's never seen or heard of before!

Can Ned really be serious? Find out in *TILL DEATH DO US PART*, Case #24 in The Nancy Drew Files℗.